GØHRIL GABRIELSEN

TRANSLATED FROM THE
NORWEGIAN BY JOHN IRONS

Peirene

Svimlende muligheter, ingen frykt

AUTHOR

Gøhril Gabrielsen, born in 1961, grew up in Finnmark, the northernmost county in Norway, and currently lives in Oslo. She won Aschehoug's First Book Award for her 2006 novel *Unevnelige hendelser (Unspeakable Events)*, and was the recipient of the 2010 Tanum Scholarship for Women. Since the publication of her debut novel she has brought out two further books to great acclaim in her native Norway, *Svimlende muligheter, ingen frykt (The Looking-Glass Sisters)* and *Skadedyr (Vermin)*. Her fourth novel is due out in 2015.

TRANSLATOR

John Irons studied modern and medieval languages at Cambridge before doing research within the field of poetic imagery. Since the mid 1980s he has translated poetry, fiction and non-fiction from the Scandinavian languages and was awarded the NORLA translation prize for non-fiction in 2007.

MEIKE ZIERVOGEL
PEIRENE PRESS

This is a tragedy about
a woman who yearns
for love but ends up in
a painfully destructive
conflict with her
sister. It is also a story
about loneliness –
both geographical and
psychological. Facing the
prospect of a life without
love, we fall back into
isolating delusions at
exactly the moment when
we need to connect.

First published in Great Britain in 2015 by
Peirene Press Ltd
17 Cheverton Road
London N19 3BB
www.peirenepress.com

First published under the original Norwegian language title *Svimlende muligheter, ingen frykt*, H. Aschehoug & Co. (W. Nygaard) AS © 2008.

This translation © John Irons, 2015.

ISBN 978-1-908670-24-3

This book is a work of fiction. Names, characters, businesses, organizations, places and events are either the product of the author's imagination or used fictitiously. Any resemblance to actual persons, living or dead, events or locales is entirely coincidental.

Designed by Sacha Davison Lunt
Photographic image by Gowangold / Alamy
Typeset by Tetragon, London
Printed and bound by T J International, Padstow, Cornwall

This translation has been published with the financial support of NORLA.

This project has been funded with support from the European Commission. This publication reflects the views only of the author, and the Commission cannot be held responsible for any use which may be made of the information contained therein.

Co-funded by the
Creative Europe Programme
of the European Union

GØHRIL GABRIELSEN

TRANSLATED FROM THE
NORWEGIAN BY JOHN IRONS

Peirene

The Looking-Glass Sisters

I

In the attic

My sister and her husband are outside, digging a deep hole next to the dwarf birch by my attic window. As they work their way down among the scrawny roots, the spade hits the earth rhythmically. They've been at it for more than an hour now. I lie motionless in my bed, listening to the sounds creeping up the thin walls of the house and into my room via the vent above the chest of drawers: the dull spade-cuts, the clanking of stone against steel, spade-cut by spade-cut down into the dry soil.

What are they looking for during this day that never becomes night? What's their business down in the depths, beneath several layers of earth? They talk quietly, don't exchange that many words. I sense a relaxed friendliness between them. Now and then they stop and fall silent. Do they sense me? The fact that I'm awake? But they only swap the spade in order to share the work equally.

As usual, they agree about everything, my sister, Ragna, and Johan.

For a while they must have gone. But then they come back, groaning and with shuffling steps. They're dragging something – the sounds betray them. It must be heavy, what they're carrying. I can see them in my mind's eye: Ragna's knitted brow, the dogged expression on her broad face, the thin arms that hold on to the load with a determined grasp. And her husband, striving to find a grip to cope with the weight. I picture him: his stomach's in the way, bloated, as it always is. He has to move with his back bent and with small, quick steps to keep up with her – always keeping up with her.

The load is heaved into the hole. Earth is thrown over it.

Deep down there, in the black hole in the ground, lumps of stone and sand and earth land on something soft. I can say this for sure from the short, dull thumps. I can feel them right next to my ear as I lie here, thump after thump, until the sounds grow fainter and close around me.

I am tired, on the point of falling asleep. Far away, I hear the earth being tidied, then covered, probably with peat and heather. Soon I am dozing dreamlessly, just as hidden as the thing down there in the dark earth.

*

Imagine an attic. Not just any attic, but one in a remote spot in a northern, godforsaken part of the world.

Here too lots of things lie packed away: all the rubbish you don't need, all the memories of a past crammed into boxes and suitcases, invisible to the outside world under a thin layer of forgetfulness and dust.

You go up there only reluctantly, and preferably not alone – it's got something to do with the creaking of the staircase so narrow and steep that you have to climb up on hands and knees. It's not easy to make it to the room at the top. And it's even more difficult to come down.

As soon as you can straighten up under the rafters, you are enclosed in dry air, but in something else as well. You wonder if it may be the darkness, the particles of dust in the strip of light from the staircase. But when you stand there perfectly calm, you know it's the stillness, the silence from the things that cannot talk, the past that lies gagged in the unceasing rush of life from the floor below and from nature just outside.

At the end of the attic there's a door. A faint light comes from the keyhole. You advance cautiously along the widely spaced floorboards that are so dry the splinters would bore into your toes if you were barefoot.

You place your ear to the door. After a moment, you sense some sound of life, not breathing and movement, but a vibration of existence, an unrest that only life can produce. You bend down, press an eye to the keyhole. It is dark. You shift position a little, move your weight on to the other leg, then bore right through with your gaze. Deep inside, among dancing white spots, you can make out the contours of a body resting on a bed. And this body, this only just perceptible unrest – it is me.

And you ask yourself, as I have done so often of late: what am I doing in this room? What's stopping me from being downstairs with Ragna and Johan? Am I being held prisoner? Am I seriously ill? Or is the being in the attic a creation of your own imagination, a frozen glimpse of the dread that chases up your spine, the fear of what you might see?

Most recently, I've had the dispiriting idea that I'm actually lying in an attic inside myself, that I am merely an old, dusty thought about living, a hidden soul that has never been allowed to go downstairs to mix and have fun with people indoors and out.

*

I don't know how long she has left me here alone. The days slide into each other, but it may well be that several have already passed, perhaps even as much as a week. How am I to know, lying here without a clock, beneath a window that lets in light from a sky that burns both day and night?

I'm dependent on her help and goodwill: she brings me my food and makes sure I put on clean clothes, takes me to the toilet and washes my body every second or third day. But she ignores my cries, does not come, punishes me severely. And repeatedly.

I have had nothing to eat or drink since I've been up here, and I've lain exhausted in bed practically the whole time. Thirst, lack of food – it's possible I can't think as clearly as before, but during the spells when I'm awake I do try to understand what has actually happened.

I'm afraid that I've become resigned that my will has been crushed and that from now on I will deny my own wishes and needs. That from now on she can decide the rhythm of when I am to eat, be awake, empty my bladder and bowels, when I am to talk, what I can say – and perhaps even what I can think. And that is what disturbs me most – exhaustion can change my thoughts, I already feel the beginnings of resignation – that from now on, without anger and resistance, I will follow her every whim and desire.

This incarceration, I view it as a blow to the very core of our relationship as sisters, an even deeper gash in the hatred. Everything that in some way has bound us together will soon be completely ripped apart.

*

Where we live is far from other people. Hardly anyone ever passed by – only the odd hare, a fox, a reindeer – until Johan moved into an old house about two or three minutes away. Some miles further west there's a small trading post where my sister and Johan do their weekly shopping. In the summer they go by motorbike, in the winter by snow scooter.

Naturally, I don't have much to do with anyone. Since I fell ill as a child, I've hardly been anywhere, and because I haven't got better, it's out of the question for me to tag along with Ragna and Johan, either to the village or to visit people. That doesn't upset me. If some poor person arrives by accident, I keep quiet in the background.

From the window of this room, which is remarkably like my room on the floor below, I can see an endless expanse of heather. I've read that it stretches right to the far side of the globe, twisting and turning through dense pine forests and round thousands of Finnish lakes before once more spreading out endlessly across the freezing-cold Russian tundra.

Even if my legs were all right, they wouldn't help me much if I wanted to see the world. To the west and north of this barren land lies the Arctic Ocean and to the east an endless expanse of emptiness. The road south to the big towns is long and tiring.

*

At first, after having been forced to move, I was agitated and full of rage. I got up from my bed to do my exercises several times a day.

I'm partially paralysed from somewhere in the middle of my back downwards. But I have no trouble getting up, as the top half of my body is strong. I turn it out towards the room, guide my legs over the edge of the bed and down on to the floor one by one, noisily, if I want her to hear me. Then I grasp the handles of my crutches and heave myself into an upright position, relying on my arms to support my withered legs. I move forward by throwing my body from side to side, working myself along the floor in the direction I want to go.

To begin with I thought my stay up here would be short. Once Ragna had become calm again she would bring me downstairs, and after making her point by not speaking to me and ignoring me for several days, everything would be as it was before: some daily confrontations, rounds of arguing and shouting at each other, the occasional fit of rage. For I want nothing more than to return to my old room and my daily rhythm, to diverting my thoughts with my dear books, to the serenity of the body when it wakes up at night or in the morning in the same old bed, with the toilet in the corridor just outside.

But I have to realize that we've come to a watershed in our relationship as sisters. After our last agonizing quarrel, it looks as if she's forgotten me. I've been stowed away like an object among all the other objects up here – discarded and outside time.

*

I sleep without dreaming, and when I'm awake I flow between different states like a quiet river. In this condition, the sounds from below are the only things I really listen to and take into consideration. But for a long time everything has been surprisingly peaceful and quiet, especially after the digging outside, and that must already be many days ago now.

How can she leave me lying here like this, and why this palpable stillness, this whispering and tiptoeing from room to room, when normally they make a racket as they talk to each other? If they think I no longer notice them, they're both wrong. For I can hear quiet, quivering conversations, chores being performed. I can pick up the sound of them squirming under the duvet and the laughter rolling back and forth between them.

But I hear more than that, for I believe I can distinguish the sound of day from evening during this time of year with no darkness, and I can distinguish the silence of sleep from the silence of my loneliness.

The tiny details, the signs of what was brewing, her final rejection and my banishment: my mirror image that is not fixed in her shiny pupils, I who am reflected back, do not exist in the darkness in there. I must have seen it coming.

II

Downstairs, a year earlier

'You've got to go.'

She's standing over me, it's morning and she says it before I'm completely awake.

'You've got to go,' she repeats, and slams the door behind her.

I've got to go. It's final, she's said it, and it means that she's decided she can't put up with having me around any longer. How far have things actually gone, I ask myself? Does she gag when she turns aside the duvet and sees my limp, thin legs? Does she burn inside when she serves me food, washes my clothes? Is she a walking vacuum, a soundless roar; is she absent from her own life because I make demands on her the whole time? And has the situation got worse since she met Johan?

She wants to put me in a nursing home in the village, that's where she wants to park me; she's threatened to do it before. I'm not very old, just partially paralysed. I've always lived here and I will never leave this house. Admittedly, this is a place where I'm invisible and away from the world, but I'm also part of everything: every splinter in the floor, every knot in the wooden boards – I know each one. Here, where the sun moves unceasingly across the sky all summer, I am more than I can dream of. And I smoulder like old firewood when the sun is below the horizon all winter. I have a special ability to cling on, to live in what is there.

The threat of being sent away comes after one of our lesser confrontations, after a mild summer evening when I go to bed early and settle comfortably among the pillows. I leaf through an old book, note a couple of thoughts in the margin, as I always do before going to sleep. The window's ajar; it's impossible to prevent a mosquito or two from getting in, despite the netting in the window frame. On my bedside table I've lit a mosquito coil and the smoke is spiralling round in gentle circles, right across to Ragna, who is standing in the doorway, wrinkling her nose. She shoves the door open with her foot, goes over to the bedside table, fumbles under the lampshade with a shaking hand and turns off the light.

'No,' I say. 'No,' I say again. 'Can't you see I'm reading?'

She doesn't answer, but takes the mosquito coil, which comes away from its foot, presses the glowing end into the saucer and crushes it into small, smoking pieces that are quickly extinguished. She waves her hand in front of her mouth, which is compressed into a thin streak.

'I've told you before,' she says, emphasizing each word. 'The smell makes me feel ill!'

I don't answer and switch the light back on. I like to have the lamp lit, even when the sun shines all night; it's got something to do with how the shadows fall in the room. Ragna breathes heavily and stretches out her arm to turn it off again, but I stop her in mid-air by grabbing her wrist. She turns away, pulls her arm out of my grasp, straightens up.

My sister, Ragna: for a moment I consider her from a place many years previously, stare at her from there towards this now, where she stands quivering with resentment, from the time when her hair was long and deep copper, and her slender neck bore the broad face with ease and a certain elegance. The point in our history where I can feel a reluctant touch of tenderness for what she was and what she became: her hair now thin wisps, her head craning out into the world on a neck of stringy sinews, the taut muscles, always ready to slash and hack.

Maybe she senses this light breeze of tenderness that moves through me, for she chews her lip and stares at me with narrowed eyes before turning and leaving the room.

I'm asleep, dreaming uneasily. When I wake I call out immediately for Ragna.

'Ragna,' I shout from the bed. 'You must come. I've got cramp!'

It's silent for a long while. She never comes at once; I always have to call out a few times. That's why I shout at the slightest suspicion of a problem with my legs: if I wait too long the pain might become unbearable before she finally gets to the door. I twist and turn under the duvet, puff and pant and moan. 'Hurry up. Come quickly. What are you waiting for?' I grab hold of her nightdress when it sweeps across my arm as she shuffles forward and pulls out the drawer of the bedside table to fetch the cream. Her face contracted, eyes closed, she fumbles blindly, mechanically, sits down on the side of the bed. I call out, 'Hurry up!' and tug at her nightdress while she spreads the cream over her hands, then finally lifts the duvet and starts to massage my thighs and lower legs, up and down, rhythmically, lazily. Her face is still blank; she grunts in time with the movements, faint snorts rising from the slumped body.

What does Ragna know about pain? She who never says anything if she hits her finger with a hammer, or traps her toe in the door, or gets stung on the cheek by a wasp. At worst, she lets out a little gasp. Ragna is armour-plated, protected against attack, impressions and impulses, despite her thin, almost transparent skin. Ragna is a person you instinctively talk loudly to, long and hard, so as to be heard through the thick layer of resistance.

'A bit harder!' I shout out into the room. 'Can't you do it a bit harder?' I yell as loudly as I can. I fling myself forward and grab her arm. She gives a start, a sleepy gasp for air escaping from her mouth. She doesn't look at me, but squeezes her fingers round my thighs, starts to rub with the firmness that may ease the cramp. When her hands have reached my lower legs, round my ankles, I think I can hear her muttering. I sense that she is completely awake, though she still doesn't look at me; there is something vigilant about her. I know that she will now toss and turn in her bed, unable to sleep, for the rest of the night.

I sink down into the pillows. There are red marks on my skin from Ragna's hands, but the cramp has gone. She pulls down my nightdress with a rapid movement, throws the duvet over me, hard and demonstratively. 'That's enough! You're not getting any more!' her face says, her entire body says, and then she stands up while breathing through her nose in that powerful, uneven way of hers that reveals she is trying to keep control of herself.

My glass is empty. I'm thirsty and would like something to drink. The water she places on the bedside table in the evening I've often drunk before the night is over. It's no real trouble for her, as I've got a washbasin with hot and cold water in my room. But I don't dare say anything, staring fixedly at the glass as she replaces the cream. She ignores my gaze, slams the drawer shut and leaves.

I hear her throw herself on to her bed with a groan in the bedroom across the corridor.

Is she lying there with her brown-green eyes open? I think I can sense her awake, her heart that pounds away in her thin body, that ever-present rage at the loss of her own life.

I imagine her lying like a black seashell in her bed, hollow but with a hard outer covering over the convoluted path to the emptiness deep inside. If I place an ear to her mouth, I won't hear anything except the distant murmur of nothing.

A nothing that sucks so strongly that when Ragna wakes up the following morning she has no other thought than to move her sister out.

*

'Have we got the strength for this?' my parents probably thought when they sat by the bed and stared at the sick child who had come to them so late in life. Until that day, they had thought of her as a guest you don't have to pay any particular attention to, a guest who takes care of her own welfare via her quite unique dependency. The daughter was almost four years old and had perhaps been a bit pale of late, but she grew and was, generally speaking, a pleasure to have around. Later, when she could hardly move her legs, her parents whispered quietly to each other that she had complained about headaches and muscle pains, but not so much that they needed to react and they had forgotten about it immediately afterwards. Children often dramatize.

She ran a high temperature and whimpered that her body felt so queer. Her old parents looked at each other, didn't know what to believe, and told her sister, who was five years older, to sit with her – they had such a lot to do themselves. The days passed as in a fog. Or was it a matter of hours? She doesn't know, she's never been given a proper answer; they always avoided the issue, went vague and speechless later when she asked them: How long? How long did I lie in bed at home before going to the hospital? She's pretty sure it was at least twenty-four hours, for she has a vague memory of her sister sitting by the bed staring at her with gleaming eyes, while the autumn sky outside changed from light to dark.

At the hospital, tens of miles away and down by the coast, her head, back and legs were examined for several weeks – perhaps months. No one remembers how long she was away and all she can recall is the absence that tingled and stiffened in her chest. Her parents couldn't stay with her, those were the rules, and they weren't allowed to come and visit her either, those were the rules too. And anyway, who would take care of the sister, the house or the sheep they owned back then? That was their excuse, at any rate, when as an adult she confronted them with her own recollection that they had simply left her behind in the hospital.

The heaviness in her heart and stomach: not the pains, the examinations, the fever and the strange people, but the nights when she woke up in a bed with high bars, when in confusion she called out for her sister and parents and nobody came, apart from the exhaustion and emptiness that gradually filled the absence of those she missed.

She started to study her fingers. She saw that there were just as many on each hand, and when she stretched them up in the air, she saw that they reached just as far as each other into the room. Her legs were withered, not yet completely numb, not two dead landscapes outside herself. If she wanted to, she could move her toes. She paid attention to the houses outside the window, the various colours, the shapes. She noticed the plank missing from a veranda, the foundation wall that was peeling, the irregular row of house roofs along the horizon and, when she lifted the duvet, the contours of her toes, the lines along her feet and up her legs, the weak curve from the iliac crest to her stomach. She sucked in everything that was firm and sure, opened herself to the surfaces, forms, lines, contours, while inside her that which breathed and sensed and moved contracted and shrank.

Her little heart. Shrivelled, like the animal hearts in the larder that her sister cooks with cream.

Just how shrivelled, how hard am I? The tears that don't come, that have to be wrung out of my eyes? The steep boundaries between what I want and don't want? The sharpness of the words?

Lies. All the lies, and I who get so worked up, ill at the thought of being sent away from this place, I who am over-whelmed by the presence of precisely these walls, who am moved by the faint murmur of the wind through precisely this crack in the window, who am moved by observing the world from precisely this room, the vast open spaces outside from precisely this spot in the world.

*

Our parents died early, one shortly after the other, and so my sister and I were left to fend for ourselves at the ages of nineteen and twenty-four. Or from Ragna's point of view: she was left with me. Or as I see it: she and I in this house, two stationary people in a constantly shifting world, the two of us holding on tight to each other. While the seasons change, the birch trees grow, while the scrub around the house thickens and the old cart road gets overgrown, our lives remain unchanged. The daily rhythm of cleaning and meals, the annual cycle with the quiet observance of mid-summer and Christmas – everything had a sleep-inducing sameness about it for twenty-nine years, right up until that day in May when Johan came to our door.

Of course our day-to-day lives have always been full of a certain drama. Seemingly ordinary events can weaken or intensify the never-ending power struggle between us. These events resemble each other and recur at regular intervals (even after Johan's appearance on the scene). They are actually so regular that I can easily describe the average one, or rather the average plot, the average course of events.

This is how things might take place between us any morning:

The crows are cawing, a wind sweeping past. I am gazing at the birch tree outside the window while Ragna is preparing breakfast in the kitchen.

'If I'm not a good sister, well, I don't know what a good sister is!' I can imagine her long, slender neck bobbing forward as she chunters on. She hasn't come into my room yet. I have shifted myself to the toilet and back; it took at least half an hour, and she didn't help me either. Back in my bed at last, I wait exhausted and impatient for something to eat, but Ragna always has a thousand things to do before starting breakfast.

'What would you like on your bread, sister dear?' she asks, using the voice she adopts when she wants to feign a certain warmth and consideration.

'Cheese.'

'Cheese it is. Cheese is good for you. Isn't it a good thing I bought the cheese you're so fond of?'

'Yes.'

Suddenly she's in the room, carrying a tray.

'Eat up, then. I'm busy. I'm going to smoke the hearts today. No point in waiting.'

She's standing in front of my bed, watching me pick up the slice of bread, open my mouth and bite.

'Well, what are you waiting for? Eat! It's cheese. And I'm busy!'

'You don't have to stand there,' I say between bites. It's difficult to chew, as I have hardly any saliva in my mouth after drinking much too little during the night.

'I want to wash up before I leave. The worktop has to be clean and ready for when I get back with the hearts. I need the space before I hang them up in the cupboard.'

I chew and chew – it's impossible to move the bread inside my mouth unless there's enough saliva to soften it and send it down to my stomach. Ragna, wearing her outdoor clothes, now fidgets by the window, staring with clenched jaws at the heather outside, but I know that her attention is fixed on my mouth, which is trying to keep shut over my teeth and the bread.

'Can I have a glass of milk?' I say after finally managing to swallow.

Ragna rushes out the room, rattles with a glass and the milk jug, is back in an instant and sticks the glass right under my nose.

'Drink!'

I have already taken another bite and my mouth is full of bread. I look beseechingly at her, point with a finger at the bulge in my cheek. She sighs impatiently, presses the glass against my lips, forces my mouth open and pours in the milk. I swallow and swallow. It's not easy, for I have to make sure that the bread doesn't slide against my palate. I grasp her hand to remove the glass, but at the same moment some crumbs tickle the back of my throat, the milk goes down the wrong way and I cough up the contents over her arm.

'You monster!'

She slams the glass down on the bedside table and wipes her arm dry on the bedclothes.

'I only want to help, but look what happens! Well, you'll just have to manage on your own!' She storms out of the room into the kitchen. I hear her rummaging around by the worktop and pouring coffee into a thermos flask with quick movements.

I pick up the lumps of bread from the bedspread and put them on the tray. I set about eating the rest of my breakfast. My chest is sodden, but I chew and chew and am about to drink the milk when she is back at my bedside again. She smiles and bares her teeth, then suddenly whisks the bread and milk glass out of my hands.

'You've finished, that's good,' she says, and places the glass on the tray.

I sit there astonished, my hands as if frozen: the one hand without the glass, the other close to my mouth without the bread. I must look ridiculous, but I stay sitting like that while listening to the clinking of the glass and tray as she goes out into the kitchen, throws away the rest of the bread and washes up. Clink, clink, like faint bells.

And in an instant she is out of the door.

*

This is how any afternoon might develop:

Ragna is resting in her room, I am in mine. Maybe we sleep for half an hour before I need to pee. I lift aside the duvet as carefully as I can, almost without a sound, so as not to wake her. But there is no way I am able to avoid breathing, perhaps panting when I sit up in bed, stop my crutches from making a rattling noise when I place them on the floor, and I am unable to prevent my nightdress from swishing when I slide down from the bed and plant my legs on the floor. When I straighten up, there can be no doubt. The creaking and cracking from my limbs and my back tell anyone that I am purposefully moving across the floor in the direction of the toilet, and now only one thing counts: to get my body moving faster, to reach a speed that can guarantee me a swift meeting with the lavatory seat well before Ragna picks up my movements. But despite all my exertions, I know from the faint rush of air across the back of my neck that the same thing as always is happening: Ragna will get there just before I do and, before I have time to protest, she will be inside the toilet and have shut the door behind her.

(This is all Ragna knows about waiting for something from a hole:

Lying on a frozen lake with a line and with one eye on the ice hole, nice and warm in a scooter outfit and on a reindeer fur. Soon the char will come, prime and plump and, within half an hour, it will take the hook. She waits, preening herself from sheer pleasure, jiggles the line a bit, maybe drinks a cup of coffee; she's waiting for the fish that's sure to come, large and red, inching its way towards the ice hole, her ice hole, smooth and deep. The water surges and falls, a cloud drifts past,

Ragna squints at the sharp winter sky and then there is a sudden jerk on the line, the fish is caught and now it is pulled up and out of its wet hiding place. Ragna smiles and seizes it by the gills, thinks of the frying pan back home as she breaks its neck – the fish, half-dead, floundering on the grainy ice; soon gutted and gleaming with fat.)

I stand outside the toilet door; heavy with a thousand lakes and ten thousand char, help me, jig, jig, there's no time to lose, the ice hole is about to burst, run over, cascades of water and landed fish!

'Ragna! Why have you locked the door?'

'Because I want some peace, you simpleton!'

'Yes, but I need to pee first!'

'No, I'm in here right now!'

'Ragna!'

'That's exactly why I lock the door, otherwise I can't get any peace!'

The water surges and falls, surges and falls, a thousand rivers feeding the lake, which fills up, drips and gurgles and flows. I can't walk, can hardly stand, can't sit down, can't lie down. I am locked, motionless, and if I move at all, the water will overflow and drown all life.

'Ragna, open up!'

I lean cautiously against the door without moving my feet and lower body, place an ear against the wood. What is she up to?

From the sound of the cistern I can make out Ragna's intermittent low breaths, small light grunts that tell me she is straining. It must be all the meat she's eaten recently, mince from the innards she cooked the other day.

I give her a little time, try to think of other things, hoping the water will recede. It has to be a mild summer's day, yes, I'll think of a mild summer's day, one with the washing hanging out, white and clean, billowing in the light breeze to the humming of the mosquitoes, the rustling of the birch trees, the babbling and trickling of the stream…

'Ragna! Get a move on!'

I hammer on the door with my crutch.

That sound inside, is she laughing? I place my ear against the door again. It's seething and bubbling in her throat, now she's letting go, and her laughter lets rip in the tiny room.

'Ragna! Ragna!' she mimics with a distorted voice. 'Ragna! Get a move on!'

All I can do is stay calm, I say to myself. Don't think of anything. Don't get upset. With these words I slide into a state of patience, and I manage to wait, for some seconds, yes, even a couple of minutes perhaps. Until I hear the sound of running water. Ragna has flushed and is now turning the taps on. She whistles loudly while letting the water run. There's no tune to it, just an echo of her hollow interior at an assumed cheerful register.

The dam gives way under the pressure and the water gushes out. It happens in a moment, but I have time to notice this dual feeling pass through my body: the pain of holding it back, the relief at finally letting go. At the same instant, I am stricken with intense sadness, the tears well up, but maybe it's the relief and not the pain, or both, but I cry and leave off, cry and leave off – it's lovely and it's sad, it's good and it's bad – I cry at myself and Ragna's gurgling laughter, at her hidden rage in every single gasp, and I cry at what is about to come – her vocal cords that will whip and lash when she discovers what misery I have caused out here in the corridor.

*

And this is how many of our mornings turn out:

I'm sitting on the toilet, the seat has warmed up and I have found the right position so as to be able to stay here until my mission has been successfully accomplished. At such times a rare calmness may come over me, and I don't count the minutes or the half-hours, the time is spent studying my cuticles and palms, the strange patterns in the plaster on the walls and, not least, whispering words and sentences that come to me, rhythmically, small verses to the sighing of the vent, the drip from the tap, the creaking of the surrounding house: hush, hush, swish swash widge wudge nudge no, swim swam blip blop baah bee…

Knock, knock.

'Get a move on!'

I stiffen. Alarm bells ring, ongoing processes are retracted. Alert, red alert!

'You've bloody well been sitting there for ages. Now you really must make way for other people!'

I sigh. All functions were on their way perfectly. If Ragna doesn't calm down soon, it will take ages to get back into the same state.

'Ragna, I'm the one who's here now!'

'Yes, damn it, you're always the one in there – or trying to get in!'

She kicks the door twice, but moves away. Judging from her steps, I work out that she has gone into her room and is lying down on her bed.

I give a sigh of relief, try to recapture that flowing calmness. It is easier than I had feared and I am in the process of drifting off on the patterns and just audible words when there's another kick on the door.

'Get a move on, I said!'

Ragna is standing with her mouth close to the door. I hear her breathing. From experience I know to keep quiet so as not to fuel her rising anger – in that way I'm able to postpone the disaster.

Ragna stays standing outside, but is not at a loss. She now starts switching the light off and on.

'Out! Out! Out!' she intones in time with the light switch.

The change between dark and light is quite intriguing, but after a while I start to get dizzy.

'Stop that, Ragna. It makes me feel sick!'

'You can puke for all I care if you don't come out quickly.'

'You don't mean that.'

'Yes, I bloody well do. You don't seem to understand that I need to use the loo too!'

Boundless conscience. There's nothing else for me to do but block my urge, forget my own needs, which have died down anyway with all this rowing.

'All right, then.'

I sigh loudly and grip my crutches, prepare myself for the laborious process of getting up and adjusting my clothes. It takes time, to be honest, even though I hurry as much as I can. And Ragna has to help me to pull up my pants, because I can't do it on my own.

'All clear!' I say, and bang my fist against the door to open it.

'You'll have to help me,' I continue, and aim for the corridor since there's more room out here for Ragna to kneel down and pull up my pants. But as I pass the door with my pants round my ankles, Ragna slips past me into the toilet. I turn round and am about to say something, but she has managed to close the door hard before I get a word out.

'You've got another thing coming,' she shouts, and laughs loudly and affectedly.

I sigh and stay standing there, feeling at that moment in my tortuous existence a slight breeze pass my bottom as the door slams shut and the shaking in my knees after all that hurrying. And when I hear Ragna giggle to herself as she finds a comfortable position on the already warmed-up seat and hear her loud grunts of pleasure, I can't help laughing a bit at it all either.

*

I must admit that Ragna and I have had a lot of good moments during our years alone in this house. But they tend to be seasonal and come with the weather – or winter, to be more precise. When the storms tug at the planks of the house, when the windows shudder and the stove wails in the fearful draughts, we get on best. In such weather the house turns ice cold and all we can do is stick to our beds. But our battle against the violent forces is a shared cause, that of keeping body and soul – and the house – together.

'I'll throw on another log,' Ragna might shout, and pad out of bed.

'Fine. We must never let the stove go out,' I call back.

'We've got to try and keep the water from freezing! You can use the toilet first,' she might say later.

'Will do!' I reply.

'Do you need an extra duvet?' I might ask.

'No, you just keep yourself warm,' she replies.

Sometimes Ragna and I even move into the kitchen. She places our mattresses right next to the stove and close to each other. 'We'll just have to make the best of a bad job,' she says, and plumps up the duvets and pillows.

At times like that, we don't look at each other but instead often exclaim things, as if to ourselves: 'One hell of a gust, that was!'

Or: 'Really wicked, that one!'

Or: 'Bloody hell! Now it's going to take the whole house!'

And then we snuggle into our duvets, turn our backs to each other, and wallow in warmth and contentment.

At times like these, in the dark, maybe with a candle lit, a sudden, intense feeling overcomes me that Ragna and I are one body, completely inseparable. We have gradually let go of parts of ourselves in favour of the other. Over the years, through conflicts and confrontations, we have shaped, kneaded and formed ourselves into a lopsided, distorted yet complete organism. Ragna has the body and I have the soul. She puts on the firewood, I do the thinking. She makes the tea, I read and write. And we both agree: God, it's cold!

*

One Thursday a couple of months ago, we were wrenched out of our day-to-day existence by someone hammering on the front door. Johan, broad and tall and with a stomach well outside the band of his trousers, does not wait for us to open and perhaps welcome him in. No, he walks straight into the kitchen where Ragna and I are sitting. Here he stands, legs apart, in front of the stove, tells us that he has moved into the house next door, which has stood empty for over thirty years, and that he has a state lease and intends to live off hunting and fishing. I listen to the conversation that develops between him and Ragna, do not ask any questions, do not ask where he comes from. It doesn't feel natural to me, and since we haven't spoken all that much since, I still don't know what he did in the years before he arrived.

Johan is a man who has come to stay. Already on his second visit he goes over to the fridge and takes some milk without asking, puts his feet up on the table and looks possessively at Ragna. Ragna lights up, brushes his feet away, immediately puts him to work.

'Can you repair tools?' she asks, she who repairs everything herself, slapping him on the back with feigned hardness.

'Course I can,' he replies, and sits down to look at the tool Ragna passes him, with half an eye on her.

He takes no notice of me as I sit silently at the kitchen table, my arms round my crutches.

The visits soon become more frequent.

Ragna bakes bread, loaves larger and more luscious than I have ever tasted, and cakes, extra sweet with a soft base.

'You're bloody good at baking,' Johan sighs, with his fingers in the latest batch.

'And you're a fat barrel that has to be filled,' she retorts.

Ragna commands. Johan works. Morning and evening he walks through our house with nails and hammer, screwdriver and saw. Four weeks after his first visit, the roof has been checked, the gutters cleared, half-rotten planks outside replaced, the window frames patched up and painted.

The sun shines through newly cleaned windows; our home smells fresh and of baking.

One day Johan comes in with a plastic bag of old clothes. He takes out a pair of trousers and holds them up against the lamp. The light can be seen through threadbare material, revealing two large holes at the back. He affectedly shrugs his shoulders, his look expressing how sad it is to own such poor clothes. Ragna grabs the trousers with a wry smile, nods to Johan to sit down and then fetches the sewing machine from the cupboard in the hallway. With nimble fingers she threads the cotton silently – displaying deep concentration as she places a piece of material over each hole and manoeuvres the trousers in under the pressure foot.

Ragna finds a comfortable sitting position and draws in her breath, presses the pedal as far down as it will go. Everything proceeds at breakneck speed, the trousers fly this way and that, in one direction and then the other, under the insistent hammering of the needle. Johan stares at the efficiency, the assuredness, the violent energy. The trousers are ready in no time. Ragna holds them up, swings them back and forth to judge the result, then throws them into his lap without a word and with a smirk on her face.

*

Already after five weeks I note that the nature of the visits has almost imperceptibly begun to change. The energetic working partnership has become more physical and direct; now it is clearly a question of looking each other over.

As, for example, the Friday Johan comes to dinner. I am also sitting at the table, my sister in the middle and Johan on her right. Ragna has covered the table with a tablecloth and decorated it with a sprig of rosebay, so I eat as tidily as I can in order not to spoil the occasion.

I don't say anything, pretend not to notice what I see and gradually understand: Johan, chuckling with a potato in his mouth, has his gaze fixed on my sister's scraggy neckline. The table rocks, the rosebay sways, Ragna's chest is bright scarlet. The kitchen thuds and thumps, divides into two worlds: what is happening above the table and what is happening below.

Or the Monday Johan comes back from town in the late afternoon with his bag full of provisions. (The previous day he had volunteered to do the weekly shopping in the village for Ragna. All that exertion and so much to carry, no, he's got a motorbike and has to do his own errands anyway.) Sweat pours off him, his rucksack is lifted down on to the kitchen floor with a groan. Ragna opens the larder, starts to unpack and stack the items on the shelves. Cold air and the smell of dried meat seeps out into the kitchen. Johan squeezes into the tiny room with her; I can see both of them from where I'm sitting in my room. From here I also watch him pulling at her sweater, lifting it over her shoulders, taking hold of her breasts, which stand stiffly apart, above her plunging neckline. Johan kneads away, my sister clucks with pleasure, then casts a swift glance in my direction before slamming the door.

And like the morning Johan comes before Ragna is up, and long before I normally surface. His steps must have woken me, and when he taps on her window, lightly and cautiously, I am wide awake. She is out of bed in a trice and lets him in, her quick movements betraying that she has been lying there waiting for him. They whisper together, imagining they are undiscovered. The front door is open, allowing a breeze to come in, and there is a slight creak from a beam overhead.

I'm asleep, I'm not asleep. I try to get back to a point in my sleep where I don't have to witness what I fear is happening. I clench my eyes tight. Johan has closed the door of Ragna's bedroom; now he's taking off her nightgown, it falls to the floor. The walls are paper-thin. I concentrate on breathing: my breath is deep and heavy, sleep breathing, regular and rhythmical. Come rest, allow me some repose, free me from my sister, who is breathing more heavily, who is sucking in breath in irregular gasps, rhythmically to Johan's suppressed moans. Now he is grasping her breasts, the old tatters of them, his great fists tearing at her flesh, which gurgles and bubbles and boils. He's already stirring away inside her, I can smell it all the way from here, the juices, the mixing slobber, my sister who's being kneaded and is fermenting. I breathe in and out, open my eyes and swallow, start to whistle the national anthem – 'Yes, we love with fond devotion this our land that looms!' – then continue, louder, more piercingly, 'Rugged, storm-scarred o'er the ocean, with her thousand homes!'

I hold my breath. I hear agitated whispering. Low yelping, my sister complaining, hands fumbling, Johan continuing; his fingers in her flesh, he pummels away at her while I whistle piercingly, shrilly, 'Love her, in our love recalling those who gave us birth!'

Something happens. Feet stumbling over each other, Johan makes a final assault, my sister in reverse, I see what I hear; her body succumbs while, with clenched teeth, she stares at the door in a rage.

I howl. Johan comes with a groan, my sister lets dry air escape from the slit of her mouth.

Silence. I lie there, my eyes shut, try to become calm, breathe gently. The door is thrown open. Ragna half-naked, quivering. Her smell above my face, the sweat of the hand that slaps my skin. I hold my cheek, look at her as she disappears, the vertebrae sticking out from her back.

*

I've always liked to think of Ragna as one of those people who find every experience disappointing, everything she sees and smells and senses; she is the sort of person who constantly longs for more, every single second. I think of her body and soul as painfully separated; there is a constant discrepancy between her dissatisfied ego, which wants more, and the body's monotony of work and rest and biological rhythms. I think that Ragna's spirit will never be satisfied within the restricting boundaries of the body, that she will always stare yearningly towards the infinity outside and inside herself. And then I think: This lack is really a longing to be gone, to cease entirely.

But something has happened. There is now expectation in her eyes, a questioning upward gaze when Johan is around. Maybe when she put her hands on his shoulders, when she leaned towards him for the first time, maybe she opted for life in that movement. Is there a sting in her breast? The certainty that her earthly sensual happiness is so brief, nothing more than an ecstatic sigh in eternity? Does, then, the thought of what will be gone – that something is over and done, even in the kiss itself – hurt more than a thousand times as much?

*

Johan. One morning when I decide to have breakfast in the kitchen, he's already sitting in my chair, eating. I place myself next to him, supporting myself heavily on my crutches, rap a bit on the chair as a sign that he is to move. Ragna's gaze wanders slightly, but Johan keeps on talking, unperturbed, doesn't turn round, reaches out for the butter and spreads large lumps over his bread.

'Damn it,' he says, 'they should have gone in for tourism. There are loads of Germans here every summer!'

Johan is sitting in my chair. The chair I most like sitting in when I'm eating. That I have to sit in if my back isn't going to hurt. But he pretends not to notice and continues.

'A bloke told me this weird story recently,' he says, slurping his coffee. 'His wife was asleep in the sun outside the house and when she woke up she was surrounded by this gang of Germans, who were pointing and speaking all at once. They didn't take any notice of her at all. And this was on her own bloody plot of land!'

I hurl one of my crutches to the floor with a crash. Johan still doesn't turn round, but he lowers his voice, says indifferently to Ragna, 'What does she want?'

'You're sitting in her chair.'

'Can't she find somewhere else to sit? Can't she bloody well see I'm eating at the moment?'

'Can't you wait a bit?' says Ragna, in my direction.

'Wait?' I say to her resignedly. 'Am I meant to wait for where I always sit?'

Johan laughs, either to me or at me, he laughs to Ragna, as if my request was some private joke.

'She's hot-tempered, that one. It can't always be easy for you, Ragna.'

'Are you blind as well as deaf?' I bang the crutch I am still holding against the floor. 'I'm standing right next to you – if you've got something to say, you can say it to me!'

Johan chuckles, takes another slice of bread, then slowly and deliberately spreads a thick layer of butter over it.

I have raised my crutch, lifted it up, and now I place the end of it, with its worn-out rubber, on Johan's wrist. He sits there, completely frozen, looking fixedly at the crutch.

'Tell your sister to get that bloody thing out of the way,' he says quietly.

Ragna gets up, grins resignedly, pulls the crutch towards her. But I don't move it just yet, the cold metal against his skin – a request to surrender. It is impossible to ignore me.

'Fucking hell,' Johan says as he quickly stands up, shoving aside the crutch with enough force to cause me to lose balance and fall backwards against the wall. I push with my hands, use all my strength, but gradually slide down the wall and hit the floor. That's more than I can take, and almost immediately my legs start to quake from the sudden exertion.

Johan wipes his mouth with the back of his hand. 'What a bloody palaver,' he says, fetching his jacket, which he'd hung over the chair.

Ragna stands there in confusion, moans in despair, is about to say something, but all she manages to do is to snatch at Johan, who twists out of her grasp and rushes past.

'Johan,' she cries out desperately. 'Johan!'

He turns round at the door, throws his arms out dra-
matically and rolls his eyes exaggeratedly towards heaven.
His whole body says that he cannot do anything, that the
problem is not him but with the human scrapheap on the
kitchen floor.

As soon as he has shut the door behind him, firmly but
with restraint, Ragna is by my side. She tugs at my arm,
shakes it, pulls and tears at it in a furious attempt to get
me to stand up. Sobbing the whole time.

*

Days and weeks go by. I glide into a soothing rhythm of
calm everydayness. It is an illusion, I know that, for beneath
the dependable surface conspiracies smoulder, along with
my sister's hot-tempered desire for her own life.

If I am to retain the right to live in this place, I must
hone such skills as vigilance and suspicion, and so as to
mark this decision, I write these skills on the palm of my
hand in capital letters.

That's a habit I have – to jot down what I am thinking.
I immediately write it down on a random piece of paper.
I battle for everything combustible in this house – government circulars, sales brochures and the newspapers that
are bought every Monday. But Ragna insists on using
everything for lighting fires.

'Can you remember to buy me a notebook?' I shout out to
her whenever she goes shopping in the village.

'Yes, yes, all right,' she shouts back impatiently, and
slams the door. At other times, I ask for books. 'Ragna,' I

say, 'can you drop in at the library on your way home?' She doesn't answer, never promises anything, but occasionally, perhaps when several months have passed, she may bring home a bag or two of books. The selection is always a surprise. I suspect her of having randomly snatched them up in passing, for they deal with topics ranging from anatomy and embroidery to the history of art and the hunting licence test. She thinks I don't particularly mind, that I don't have any special favourites. And she's quite right, I read everything; that's the way I've got to know about the world.

Meanwhile, as I'm waiting for paper to write on and new books, I secretly scribble in our ten volumes of the reference work *Home University*, and I even occasionally read through the old schoolbooks and novels that our parents ordered from a catalogue when Ragna and I were teenagers and they wanted to give us some sort of 'education'. The books are in my possession – I keep them under the bed; Ragna has never shown any interest in them. So that's how I've been able to fill page after page of *Home University*, the margins, all the spaces between the lines, the white in-between pages, with everything I've thought and felt over the years. I learned to read and write from my parents, but especially from Ragna, who used to be fetched by taxi on certain days of the week and driven to school at the trading centre. It was very tiring – from the crack of dawn to late evening – and after a few years a kind of home-teaching system was devised: Ragna sitting at the kitchen table, grappling with maths problems that made my parents shake their heads in despair. No, you'd better help your sister to read and write instead.

*

Words. They can still make me feel dizzy, even so many years after I first made their acquaintance. But when I cautiously started to change their order in a sentence the dizziness became an obsession. I experienced falling into the deepest well or abyss just by moving a subject, an object, a verb around and changing one or two small words here and there:

> *My sister and I live on our own, the way to the man in the next house seems slippery and muddy.*

> *Our man slippery and muddy lives in my sister's house, I'm in the way, on my own it seems.*

I steered clear of this game for many years. Then I began to play it again. I dismantle and rebuild for hours. I don't know why. I feel intoxicated, shake and tremble – and I can't stop doing it.

*

And my sister? What does she write on her own private sheets of paper that she will never share with me? What complaints does she jot down about her exertions? I realize at once that I don't care about her complaints. But I would care if they became a letter, a letter that was completed and sent, or if a blank sheet of paper was left lying there, quivering in expectation at the words that were to be formed.

Yes, there must be papers, an application, a confirmation of what she is planning. Can an envelope of special interest have been put in our letter box at the trading post? Can I have failed to notice that Johan, after one of his four or five trips, has come back with the letter she has been waiting for? Can I have overheard the small scratch of agitation in his voice when he flings open the door and shouts: Post! And when they sit down at the kitchen table with a cup of coffee to sort the bills from the ads, can I have failed to notice the tense whispering between them when a particular envelope with the county authority's elegant stamp is torn open, the suppressed jubilation after quickly reading such sentences as: 'Your sister has hereby been approved for a place at our nursing home... She will be fetched by our ambulance team at the end of the month... We fully understand your difficult situation and hereby guarantee that your sister has been granted lifelong care...'?

Have these words been read in my proximity without my noticing the ill-will that surrounds them, the cold they release into the room? I feel like hitting myself. It strikes me as a possibility that I have dully and indifferently witnessed the planning of my own deportation.

I sharpen my senses. Follow Ragna's daily activities with apparent lack of interest from the sidelines, stay more often in the kitchen, keep my bedroom door open and an ear cocked to everything taking place out there: the sound of drawers opening, paper rustling, pen being put to paper.

I listen out for possible telephone calls. But everything is as usual, and there is just that sentence quivering between us: You've got to go.

*

Ragna is only out of the house on rare occasions, when she goes to the village, which happens less and less now that Johan has taken over the weekly shopping. When she does go, I have my only time alone in the house. Then I take over all the rooms.

I like to look through her drawers – the smell of the wood and a musty tinge from her clothes. Here I find the reverse image of Ragna. Everything she takes care of tells me something different from what is expressed between us. The lace handkerchief, elegantly laid out around the brooch that has two stones missing, the amber ornaments, the old bottle of perfume that's turned rancid: Ragna's dreams of something better and finer, dancing and grand parties.

It's the second Monday in August and, surprisingly, Ragna has gone off with Johan to the village. She announced this after my morning care. I pretended to ignore it, frightened of revealing my expectation, the agitated tingling sensation at the thought of being alone – to rummage through her things, perhaps find a letter from the nursing home, the draft of an application.

After waiting for a while, I am inside her room. I poke the door with my crutch, pull a chair over to the dresser, sit down, open the drawers, enter the forbidden land of Ragna.

All the contents are old acquaintances: every nightdress and sock, every jersey and pair of tights. Her jewellery, the long amber necklace and ear clip. Not for the first time do I preen myself in the mirror above the dresser. And once again I perceive this image of Ragna staring at her own perfect mirror-image, the jewellery that confirms her daily sacrifice, that she could have been a woman in a finer, more glamorous world.

In the bottom drawer I find a white box I haven't seen before. I place my hand on the lid, let it lie there for a while before lifting it off. The contents are red, the material shimmers in my hands: a thin nightdress, a bra and – I don't understand it to begin with – a tiny pair of panties. At the bottom, underneath the shimmering material, there lies a silver case: a crimson lipstick that smells sweet.

I hook up the bra, pull it over my head and down over my blouse. I do the same with the panties, bend down and pull them up over my trousers, lift my backside a bit in my chair, pull the elastic until it fits round my hips. I heave myself up and, with one hand on my crutch, I grab the lipstick and smear it on my lips with my face close to the mirror.

So this is Ragna. Her white body in red underwear. Johan must have ordered it – the cups are distinctly arousing, they bulge out, begging to be filled. Ragna is utmost poverty, a lifelong lean year, but Johan is hungry. If nothing else, the packaging stimulates the appetite.

Supported by my crutches and wearing Ragna's bra and panties, I move from room to room to flaunt myself. I take a leisurely cup of coffee and eat the biscuits that Ragna has laid out before leaving, I open the front door so as to be gaped at by birds, heather and moor, I display myself to the lavatory, to all the things in my bedroom and hers. Gradually, I make her red secret pale, dull and my own – something Ragna doesn't know. And in this way there is a shift in the balance of power in the space of just a few hours. I know everything about her little fairy tale, and she knows nothing about mine.

*

This erotic side to Ragna makes me wonder if her life – all these years in loneliness – has actually been as dull as I have tended to believe. For there's no denying it, something jars in the way she behaves when meeting Johan. This abandon, this moral decline, the way she crudely and freely indulges in physical intercourse, they do not suggest an inexperienced woman. It's possible that this sudden wantonness is merely biological, that it has lain dormant and unexpressed in her, waiting to be woken by the right man. But, and this is my theory, it may well be that she has become increasingly aroused as the result of a number of shameless encounters. It may well be that for several years now Ragna, on her trips to the village, on her weekly visits to the shop and the post office, exploited the opportunity to unleash the desire that had built up in the course of a long, strenuous week of nursing and domestic duties, and that on this day in the week she let it all go, her clothes included, that she lay down in a house, a home, with some acquaintance or stranger, giddy and playful, just like the hunting dogs we had for a short period.

Can I have overlooked situations like this one:

Ragna, who, flushed with excitement and expectation, places small and secret objects in her bag, things intended to seduce, to arouse desire? Ragna, who shouts 'Back soon!' with a rusty voice, short of breath from the blood pounding inside her, who says, 'See you later!', full of hidden urges? Ragna, who, heavy with lust, calls out, 'I'll be back just after eight!'

And, God help me, I can almost see it: Ragna, who for twenty-nine years runs light-footedly among the taut, sap-filled birch trunks, along the muddy country road towards the open expanse of emptiness and who there, blood-sated and dazzled, panting, imagines the hours ahead of her.

'Yes, master! I'm ready for anything!'

*

Back in the chair in her room, and having returned the underwear to where it came from, I start to wonder about Ragna's real reason for going to the village. This sudden decision to leave – she's been gone for several hours. Is she doing some serious shopping? A new snow scooter? I make a mental list. She needs a new coat, possibly some kitchen equipment. But there is really only one explanation for my uneasiness: Ragna is of course meeting with the staff of the nursing home.

I see it all: Ragna is probably sitting at this moment wringing her hands, on the very edge of the chair in the principal's well-scrubbed office.

'Please be so kind as to help me,' she says in a weak voice. 'I'm completely worn out. You can imagine it yourself: never any help, my work set out every day from morning to evening!'

The principal nods sympathetically, hands her a glass of water to encourage her to go on. Ragna swallows and tries to pull herself together, makes an effort to keep back her tears, but is surprisingly down-to-earth and clear in her account.

'My sister is much worse on her legs, the spasms have increased and she often wakes up with cramp at night. She needs help for practically everything, even the most intimate arrangements,' she says, brushing away the tears gathering in her eyes.

'What do you mean, the most intimate?' the principal asks gently.

'I have to wipe her behind,' is the meek reply. 'She can't manage that any longer.'

'And?' the principal says searchingly, encouraging her to continue.

Ragna swallows again and averts her eyes.

'It's the fault of the spasms. When she wipes herself she sometimes falls to the floor, and, well… you can imagine.' She lowers her gaze, shy like a young girl, studies her hands.

The principal takes a deep breath and straightens up.

'Terrible,' she says, shaking her head. 'But I gather that is not the worst thing?'

'No!' Ragna says with a sob that causes her voice to break. 'The worst thing is that she has become so suspicious and aggressive! She rummages in my things and flails around with her crutches for no reason!'

'How awful, how unbelievable,' the principal says, and exchanges a concerned look with the nurse who has appeared and is wiping the sweat from Ragna's brow.

Meanwhile, the principal fishes out a sheet of paper that she stamps with great authority and energy. She places the sheet on a shelf marked 'Admissions', rises and strikes the table with both hands.

'There's no doubt at all that you must have help! I've never heard of a worse case. Not only is your sister becoming increasingly disabled, but she also shows every sign of mental confusion. We will offer you all the support and assistance you need, Miss Ragna, from today!'

*

'Come on, open the door!'

Someone is hammering on the front door. I've locked it. What else can I do? I'm lost, my time's over. Through the window I've seen Ragna and Johan arriving. And it's worse than my worst fears: they are accompanied by three powerful men.

'What on earth are you up to? Open up, I said!'

Ragna shakes the door. Johan swears in the background.

'It's not that simple!'

'What do you mean?' she answers angrily.

'To get rid of me.'

'Pull yourself together. What are you babbling about?'

'I won't do it. I'm not moving!'

'Open the door, damn it!' she says, shaking the handle.

'Those men,' I try to say, placing my mouth close to the wood. 'You've fetched help,' I whisper softly.

Ragna kicks the door. Her voice is sharp.

'What the hell are you talking about? These are Johan's mates from Finland!'

'Finland? They're from the nursing home.'

'Are you ill? Unlock the bloody door.'

'You don't fool me.'

She kicks the door again in reply and steps away, then starts talking to Johan. I place my ear up close. There's something that doesn't seem right. I can hear Ragna and Johan heatedly discussing things, but without any inter-ruptions from the three men, who are standing talking a language there's no mistaking.

'Ragna,' I say, banging on the door. 'Ragna! Who are these men?'

Ragna comes back and places her mouth close to the door.

'They're from Finland, like I just told you. They're old workmates of Johan's. They're here to put up a house for a building company and he's invited them over.'

Ragna's furious, so furious that what she says must be true. Het up and confused, but also suddenly frightened about the consequences of having insisted something else was going on, I turn the key in the lock. Ragna heaves at the door before it's fully open. Her jaws are clamped shut, and if we'd been on our own she'd have hit me now, as she passes me. Johan follows immediately behind. He's really mad and he hurries after her into the kitchen. The Finns are clearly at a loss. They stand there, stamping their feet and spitting on the ground. I quickly register that two of them are Johan's age, perhaps because of their weight, but the other one, a scrawny little bloke, must be a bit younger. Johan calls to them and waves them in. They enter reluctantly, distrustfully, nudging each other when they discover me up against the wall in the corridor.

'Jee-zus,' one of them mutters as they pass.

Ragna makes pancakes, the smell filling the house; a thin film of moisture now covers my bedroom window. I lie on my bed, listening to what's taking place out there – Ragna and Johan, who are having guests for the first time. Conversation is halting, reduced to short sentences and words of one syllable, and I assume – since I can't see them from the bed – full of facial expressions and gestures.

Laughter comes easily. It takes only a word or two for loud guffaws to hit the wall. I smile indulgently, think that it would hardly be as amusing if I weren't in the next room, that they are idiots and charlatans who are trying to outdo each other showing off.

The noise level increases: the sound of sizzling from the frying pan, the clattering of plates and cutlery being laid out, feet shuffling, chairs scraping against the floor, huffing and puffing, hands that grip and let slip. I've never heard a racket like it. I shut my eyes, transform the sounds into pictures so that I can more easily follow what is going on out there, search for a reason for the visit: Finns, what are they doing here, when it comes to it?

'Can I invite you men to partake of some rather decent firewater?' Johan asks.

'*Vitun hyvää*,' the Finns answer.

The cork is rolled off the bottle with a flat hand in a rapid movement, it's easy to hear. It falls to the floor and rolls round. Cupboards are opened, glasses set out, drinks poured. There is much swilling and toasting, clearing of throats and contented sighing.

Ragna approaches the table, the men grab their cutlery, stick forks haphazardly into the pile of pancakes.

'*Helvetin hyvää*,' says one of the Finns with his mouth full.

'*Helvetin hyvää*,' the two others agree, and toast Ragna and Johan.

After the meal, the men dig out a pack of cards. While they try to agree on a game and on rules, Ragna disappears unnoticed into her room. Through the thin wall I hear her pulling out a drawer; it must be the bottom one, for now she's lifting the lid off the white box.

My heart hammers with shame and anxiety on my sister's behalf. There's a rustling of fabric, more huffing and puffing. Oh, God, now she's putting on the bra and smearing her lips with red grease. After a short while she's out of the room. I can't see her from the bed I'm lying on, but a strong whiff of partying and the promise of an available woman seep all the way to my bedside.

One of the Finns catches sight of Ragna and gives a loud whistle.

'Madonna!'

The laughter resounds, there is a chinking of glasses and more toasts.

'My woman! My wifey!' Johan yells.

Ragna giggles nervously, the scraggy bag of bones, with not an ounce of shame in her. She's given a seat at the table and a glass is put in her hand, and now she's knocking them back; I can hear from her swallowing how her throat is greedily working away. The cards are shuffled and dealt. Ragna expresses her delight at her hand, one of the men grunts, there's more drinking, slurping, the card game's started.

An hour passes. The first enthusiasm has died down, the roars of laughter are more infrequent, tension has built up. A chair is shoved hard against the wall, the legs tilt from the floor. One of the men gets up and trudges across the kitchen, opens the door to the corridor with a bang, then the front door, and outside, under a sky that's turning grey, he relieves himself over the heather with contentment and low moans.

Johan is drinking, he's the one pouring liquor down himself, and the conversation between him and the Finns suddenly grows quiet and intense. And Ragna? It must be Ragna who gets up so suddenly that a chair falls over. She heads to the worktop and turns on the radio, tries to find a channel with music.

The voices have dropped to a mumbling bass, the music stops me from making out the words; they're talking about something outside, but all I can hear is the sharp accent of the Finns, along with Johan's and Ragna's familiarly pitched voices.

Clothes in motion through the air, unsteady feet across the floor. Why aren't they talking any longer? And this rustling – is it paper being spread out? The silence inside gives way to a sudden noise of repressed sounds that rise up from every nook and cranny: the wind sighs heavily against the window frame, there's a trickling from the stream outside, the rippling must be coming from the bogs and the small suggestion of a whimper must be the door of my room, which is vibrating almost invisibly from the unaccustomed pressure that is building up from the breathing of many people.

Sounds and images merge – first the one, then the other – and it almost makes me shake my head, it's hardly credible: from what I can hear, the thing that must be happening is that Ragna has lain down on the kitchen table and pulled up her skirt, and she's now letting each of the men take her in turn, and during all this Johan is proudly observing the proceedings.

What moral decline. What depravity – and in our own home! Ragna is as if transformed, utterly bewitched. What can't such behaviour lead to? Yes, I already fear the worst, the consequences, if she continues with her sexual excess in future: possessed by drink and lust, she will abandon herself to every newly discovered desire and go off with men, never to return. After a while, she'll end up a drunken wreck on some sofa in Finland, servicing randy Finns all day long in every conceivable set of undergarments – yellow and blue and red and with cups that are far too big. And then the tragic finale: Ragna in the arms of the Finns and Johan, through hot nights that become years, while I lie rotting in this bed, slowly, little by little, in this dreadful spot that will become overgrown and disappear from the rest of the world.

I know it, my fate's already sealed, I'll end up as food for mice, rats, birds and carrion. Soon I'll be fertilizer for cloudberry moors – and what cloudberries! Pink heads, the German will think, the illicit picker, and pop the berry into his mouth. The mosquitoes will dance. The juice, the small pearls of moisture that make the German's nose quiver, is nothing but molecules of my acidic corpse fluids that will soon mingle with his sweet blood.

In the midst of this whirl of thoughts, this picture of my future life, I get a sudden sinking feeling in my stomach: the rustling paper I've just heard – of course, it's obvious, how could it be anything else? They're planning to have me sent away, that's what they're doing, the cunning bastards. They must be writing the plan down, word by word, step by step, how it's to be done. That's why the Finns are here. Johan's accomplices, his companions!

This eagerness, this low-pitched talking: they're busy planning now, their proposals are clear and definite. Everyone's contributing; even the Finns in their broken language are driven by reasons I do not yet understand.

'It's got to be winter, when the going is firm. Then it'll be easiest to get her out of here. During summer the path to the main road's much too muddy and bumpy.'

'We'll have to lash her to the scooter.'

'If she kicks up a fuss, we'll have to sedate her.'

'With what? How do we fix it?'

'Ragna will have to go to the doctor in the village, complain about aches and pains.'

'Right.'

'All of us are needed. She's not easy to handle, she knows how to lash out, the little troll!'

'We'll take a spade.'

'And then it's party time.'

'*Helvetin hyvää!*'

My heart's pounding. My forehead's throbbing.

'Ragna,' I say. 'Ragna!'

My body feels numb, only my lips are moving – they open and shut independently of me. But she doesn't hear me, my voice doesn't reach them, doesn't get through the music.

'Ragna,' I roar, shouting as loud as I can.

It goes completely silent. Not a breath, not a grunt from the men.

Someone shuffles across the floor and turns the radio off.

'Yeeeaah!'

It's Ragna, her voice distorted, coming from somewhere deep in her throat she's never spoken from before.

'Yeeeaah!' she roars from the depths once more.

I'm completely at a loss. What am I to say?

'Ragna,' I shout, and then swallow. 'Have you remembered to buy that notebook for me?'

Occasionally, in a state of deep despair, I have called on God, but the truth is that in everyday life I dismiss him as being not all that credible.

Even so, I can't deny that I have often sensed a certain presence, and as a reflection of this a sense of being reconciled to the transitory nature of life. At such moments I have had a feeling of waking up, or of just suddenly knowing that everything passes. But God is. And my soul likewise.

Have I, with this realization, any reason to fear anything?

Why, then, am I so afraid of the catastrophe: of having to leave, be gone?

'Notebook?'

Ragna gives a snort.

'She's asking about a notebook,' she says, turning to the men with a voice that wobbles a bit.

'Notebook!' she shouts in an affected voice out into the room.

There is scattered laughter from the men, someone tops up glasses, they toast and laugh again, but not unrestrainedly. They are obviously engaged in more serious matters.

'The door,' one of the Finns says in his heavy accent. 'Shut the door.'

Shuffling steps across the floor, heavy breathing just outside the room, I recognize Ragna behind the liquor and the drunkenness. She shuts the door.

'Ragna?'

I don't particularly like my voice – I'm whining. But she's already back with the men, the door's closed, the radio's on and I'm cut off from the impressions that can tell me what they are up to out there.

I often lie with my door shut. I often shut it myself. But to be shut in by Ragna, that's something quite different. I'm in the process of accepting her authority to decide the position of the door. At the same time, though, I feel resistance, as always when she forces me to accept her will, short-tempered and unshiftable.

My hands folded, I note in silence that it is impossible to overlook me, precisely because I exist. *I exist.*

I sit up angrily in bed. Full of this clarity of vision, this strength, I feel a sudden urge to assert my right of self-determination. I pick up one of the crutches, hold it in the air and shout.

'I'm here!'

'I'm here!' I shout again as loud as I can. 'And I'm bloody hungry!' I scream, bashing the crutch against the wall.

I can't help being startled at this outburst, this sudden expression of hunger, because I haven't felt like food the whole evening. But the insistence of my stomach is there now and I probably haven't eaten for four or five hours.

Ragna's face at the door.

'You'll have to wait!' Her eyes are burning, there are red, flaming patches at her neck.

'There's nothing to wait for – I'm hungry!'

I get up from the bed and, supported by my crutches, totter over to the door and tug at the handle. Ragna holds back.

'Sister!' She's at a loss, her voice slips. 'I know you're hungry,' she says, 'but you'll get something a bit later, straight afterwards. I'll rustle something up when the Finns have gone.'

Dregs of words, tangles of sentences. Her mild tone of voice jars – she could at least speak clearly and distinctly.

'Wait a moment!' I hear her shuffle back into the room and talk to the men, who answer with grunts and groans.

I don't wait, wrench open the door.

What predictable play-acting. They're all sitting there, the men and my sister, fully dressed at the kitchen table, with their liquor glasses in their hands and a vague expression of disgruntlement. I don't believe them, what hypocrisy: they've obviously got dressed quickly and cleared away the papers. I, for my part, haven't considered revealing my suspicions, everything I've understood, and root around in the bread bin, unconcerned and with complete naturalness.

But although the mind is strong, the body is far weaker. Soon I'm shuddering, my arms and legs are shaking, and it's all I can do to stay upright on one crutch, for I need the other hand to search for food. I usually don't stand here at the worktop; for the last few years Ragna has prepared the meals. I rummage around and can't find the butter. Or the cheese slicer.

After fumbling back and forth for a while, I begin to see myself as they must see me. And if I turn my head slightly I can see myself too – the face in the mirror above the sink is mine. Oh, let my pride bear me up, keep me standing, my will straighten me up, for I am truly a pitiful sight. Is that what the Finns see? An emaciated creature of feminine origin, degenerated, mutated at the edge of the wilderness? A furry animal with bared canine teeth, snarling at the smell of strangers?

I exist. So pitiable and pathetic. I have swaggered out armed with two perverted words that suddenly fall to pieces, ashamed of their own alleged strength. I regret this, change the statement to a stuttering *I exist?*, for that's the state of affairs now, with me clutching my crutches and whimpering, 'Ragna, help me.'

'What the hell's she making a song and dance about?' Johan asks.

Ragna tosses her head, empties the last dregs and puts the glass down hard on the table. She reels over to the worktop, starts to slice bread and immediately afterwards sticks a dish right up under my nose.

'Eat!'

The bread's got no butter and the salami has evidently been lying around sweating on the cutting board for several hours. I don't like salami, it's pure bloody-mindedness to put it on the bread, what is she thinking of? The greasy piece of meat suddenly symbolizes all her inconsiderateness. She expects me, then, to go the entire evening without food, to sit quietly in my room with a raging hunger, to be thankful for anything at all. There's no doubt that Johan is her main priority now, that she doesn't think about anyone else but him.

'That's my chair.'

I stand at the worktop and with my crutch hit the chair Johan's been sitting on all evening. I've shoved the plate right in front of him, between the bottles and the glasses. The Finns follow the situation with raised eyebrows and expressionless eyes, look first at me, then at Ragna and Johan. I hit the chair again. I'm so close I'm almost breathing down his neck, which folds into two thick sausages, so close that I notice the hairs sticking out from his shirt, the worn material over the meaty back. He sits motionless, his arms crossed on the table, doesn't move a muscle.

'I want to eat.'

To underline that I mean business, I raise one of the crutches, lower it slowly over the table and shift a liquor bottle that's close to the plate, slowly remove the crutch and return the tip to the floor. I do it as slowly as I can and with strength I scarcely possess. My legs are shaking, I'm breathing heavily, but now I am showing I demand my right to the chair and a seat at the table. One of the older Finns, a dark bloke with green, close-set eyes, smiles slightly. This sets a chain reaction in motion: soon the upper lips of all three of them start twitching, a twisted grin they try to restrain so as not to provoke Johan.

And Ragna? Ragna has shrunk to a small girl, wringing her dry hands while glancing across at Johan, who now lifts his backside slightly in order to find a more comfortable position on the chair.

'Ragna,' he says calmly, almost gently, turning slowly towards her, 'can't you get that bloody nuisance out of here?'

Ragna looks around helplessly, unable to deal with the unexpected situation.

'Johan,' she begs, trying to appeal to something in him, perhaps to the words he has whispered into the pit of her throat in the heat of their embrace, words that have given her the sense of a bond between them, something so strong that it can cope with a certain amount of testing. She is about to say more, but Johan interrupts her.

'Can't you just ask her to stay away while there are people visiting? She embarrasses all of us.' He pauses, looks questioningly at her. 'Don't you agree, Ragna?'

Ragna replies by tipping her head to one side and rubbing her eyes. Is it my previous episode with Johan that she is thinking of, when he flew out of the door in a rage?

'Just get the hell out of here, Johan,' I say before she has time to open her mouth. 'And take these louts with you!'

I raise my crutch and point at the Finns, who glance irresolutely at each other. Johan lifts his backside uneasily, then settles it down into the seat of the chair once more.

'Well I bloody never,' he says, staring at Ragna. 'Haven't you thought of reacting in some way?'

But I'm the one who reacts, several seconds before Ragna manages to even think the thought. I bring the crutch down on the table with all the strength I possess, sweep it from side to side so that bottles and glasses and slices of bread fly off in all directions.

'*Saatana!*' one of the Finns shouts.

The table stands in the direct line of fire and the force of the explosion causes all those sitting there to fling themselves backwards. I bash the table with all the strength I possess, I strike and strike until I notice at one point in my fury that the crutch is bending. I'm injured, the crutch, my arm and foot are injured. I have to give up, step back. And at that moment I collapse on to the floor.

Ragna is standing close to the worktop, muttering, the Finns have squeezed into a corner by the door, but Johan stands at the table, self-assured, his feet well apart, his fists clenched.

I myself am lying in a jumble of crutches, arms and legs. I try to collect my body to orientate myself, to get up, but I'm rattling and clattering away worse than our old birch tree in a storm.

'She's frigging dangerous, Ragna. There's more strength in the little monster than all of us put together,' Johan says with contrived calm.

He goes over to Ragna, places himself in front of her.

'I'm not staying here a minute longer than necessary,' he says harshly. 'Ragna, I am…' He pauses, takes a breath to emphasize the force behind what he is about to say: '…sick, yes, that's what I am, sick and tired of your sister, who exploits you and sucks the very life out of you.'

While he stands at the front door, waving to the Finns as a sign that it's time to adjourn to his cabin, he concludes, 'And the worst thing of all, Ragna, is that you let yourself be exploited, that you bloody well put up with everything.'

In *Home University*, Vol. II, 'Earth, Plants, Animals', in an empty space on page 76, I write down some sentences that occur to me early the next morning: 'My sister's a scavenger that secretly eats straw in bed, the man gives her bones to gnaw on, keeps her on a lead.'

*

'Ragna! You've got to help me!'

I'm out of breath immediately, even a few words take their toll. I'll just have to face up to the reality of the situation: yesterday's physical exertions have drained whatever strength I had. I lie huddled up in bed and my voice sounds disembodied, a braying that can only arouse Ragna's revulsion.

I'm in pain; I'm aching from my lower back right up to my neck. I couldn't find a comfortable position during the night and when I pinch my leg it's as if I'm doing so through a thick layer of material, my flesh hardly registers a thing.

Ragna has already been awake for hours and is rushing about noisily doing the housework with hectic intensity. While she washes clothes in the tub that she has placed on the worktop (my panties, she usually threads them on one hand while she rubs soap into the crotch with the other – anyone can see the stains in the white material, which means me, and sometimes Johan, and we have on more than one occasion sat in silence watching) she answers my shout by repeating her own self-defence time and time again.

'You think we were talking about you, you conceited worm, but we were talking about far more important things!' she says, while heaving the clothes out of the tub, pouring out the water, fetching the clothes horse.

I don't answer, haven't asked what they were talking about either, but when she was inside my room and threw clean clothes on my bed I suggested she was pleased with the plans made during the visit the day before.

'You little beast, you've frightened Johan off,' she replied harshly. 'If you've any sense, you'll do well to keep your trap shut.' She then gave my bed a kick before disappearing out of the door.

After a while she starts talking to herself about something completely different, and from time to time, without my having said a single word, she calls out to me to shut up. Suddenly, she bangs the mop hard against the floor and exclaims, 'The deliberate misrepresentations in this country – I won't put up with it!'

She puts the washtub down so hard on the floor that the water splashes out.

'Soon we won't even be allowed to use the roads either, we'll be hunted like stray dogs, the whole lot of us. That was what we were talking about yesterday by the way, for your information. And then you come along, with your noise and commotion, and make trouble!'

Now she's pushing the long-handled broom around the floor, bashing it into corners and along walls.

'No, you really must stop all your yelping,' she says, out of breath, 'for there are other things to think about for a poor woman who from now on will have to steal around the moors like a common thief. I who was born here just as much as they were, Mum and Dad too for that matter, they wore themselves out in this spot for half their lives, and then the damned natives claim that I don't belong here! No, our rubbish is clearly not as fine as their rubbish! Our forefathers have clearly not decomposed in the ground for as long as theirs! No, for we are bloody bandits from elsewhere, unwelcome, aliens!'

Ragna's rage floods out into our small house, rises high and higher, it presses and roars in my ears so I can hardly breathe.

'The moors that I have walked over since I was a little girl,' she intones while she moves things, pushes things around, puts things away with great violence inside the kitchen. 'My livelihood each and every autumn! From now on I'll have to stand and watch them fill their pails – and they've the whole area to take from. The government will give them everything, yes they will, Johan says. As if it wasn't just as much our refuse as theirs that nourishes the cloudberries! Let me tell you – they'll just have to spit on me when I come, fetch their rifles too, I don't care, at least I'll die on my own moor!'

She interrupts herself with a fit of coughing, but goes on in a hoarse voice, 'I've got to say it, but you keep quiet about it being said. Johan had with him a secret map of which families will take over the various areas here. And it's not us, I can tell you that! You whine like a dog for food, but soon there won't be any food around, for your further information! You ought to be ashamed of yourself and find out more about what's happening instead – for we're being ambushed!'

Suddenly she's a lot less het up.

'The right of disposition of the outlying areas, something like that, that's the fine name they give to it. When our lease from the state expires, when the new master race decide things, then, then it's all over and out with you too, you miserable worm.'

You miserable worm. She's hardly even able to say the words. They come as a final kick from a woman already on the floor, completely exhausted and overpowered.

For one weak moment I'm capable of believing her. But I quickly realize that this is due to exhaustion and repressed fear. This sudden threat of a superior force and being shut out of the moors is nothing but a distortion of the truth: I'm the one who is going to be ousted, by a master race consisting of Johan and Ragna, and I'm the one who's going to be subjected to a new regime – at the nursing home, to be precise.

The lie's good. She almost believes it herself, and maybe there's a hint of truth too. But the rage, all the force of the emotional outburst, is directed at me, and I'm quite certain that I was one of the victims of yesterday's many conspiracies.

*

Just think if I was unfortunate enough to go on living down through the centuries in the form of a series of existences – first a sparrow, then a wasp, after that a tree, a birch, and then to become a dog, a beetle and a human being again. Instead of letting my soul remain here, which is my greatest wish, I would be diluted, spread out into all kinds of states in all kinds of places, and when I eventually return, this place and I would be strangers to each other. Nothing would be recognizable, no small stone or tree.

I bend down and fish out one of the books that is lying in the dust under the bed, to be specific one of the reference works in *Home University*, Vol. III, 'Geography'. On the back cover I write, 'Let me be spared from living several lives.' And beneath, at the very edge of the margin, 'Just let me fertilize the moors.'

In real life I'm a person made for permanent, eternal states. Marriage would perhaps have been the right thing for me. A connection and obligation for ever. For isn't it the case that on the few occasions when I have left the house I immediately long to be back home? Every step, every metre I put behind me, I am distancing myself not only from home but from myself. I become roomless, hollow, without roof and walls. And as I turn round, the relief, the sight of the house, everything that step by step returns and becomes alive again. And when at some point on the way back I am reunited with myself and embrace my domestic happiness, I start to laugh. How long have I been away – five minutes?

To be quite honest, why all this talk about being composted in earth and moor? I who am never outside? Even Ragna is hardly outside the door for long periods. In the summer, the mosquitoes chase us indoors; in the winter, there is the cold and the wind.

When Ragna was young, she met a man from the south at a mountain cabin out on the plateau. Apparently he remarked that she was lucky to live in the midst of this magnificent scenery, that she certainly must have many fine outdoor experiences every single day. Ragna always grins when she tells the story, and I can well understand that: for us who are indoors most of the time, nature is simply something that takes place outside the front door – mosquitoes that come and go, and stunted birch trees that come into leaf in spring and shed their leaves in autumn. No, it's nothing to get all spiritual about. It's actually the house, my room, that I don't want to leave, and I would rather rot under the floorboards than on the boggy moorland.

To be quite honest once again, why do I insist on this urgent need to stay put? On the radio I hear about people who have to leave their homes at great speed, their own country, people who disappear, vanish, fleeing across mountains, seas and dangerous borders. To escape threats and persecution. Chased away from their work, family, bed, the cup in the cupboard.

What have I got to lose? Nothing more than my own screwed-up existence. But even that is too dear, too good, to be abandoned.

Now that Ragna has become one of those who fear having to move, will she understand my wish to stay? Will we work things out, now that the threat of banishment has become part of her life? Will we become two sisters who fix each other's hair and do each other's nails? Will I hold out a skein of wool while she winds it into a ball?

Out with the ointment and antiseptic, bandages and plasters – we're a little family with pus and pain in our cuts and scratches.

*

I dream that Ragna is standing by the seashore, on a beach with fine silver grains of sand, not unlike the shore of one of the lakes near here. She is standing on a large stone, warm in the sun, fishing with calm, slow movements, unaware that I am standing in deep water further out, waving to her.

'Catch me!' I implore her. 'Haul me in!'

I signal as best I can, with my arms and hands. But Ragna goes on casting without getting any nearer to me, while her catch grows bigger and bigger: great heaps of cod and coley. I begin to tire of signalling to her, my feet are sinking deeper and deeper into the soft seabed, and large fish steal round my body, ready to attack at the slightest sign of weakness. Finally, though, there is a tug at my flesh, the hook has caught a firm hold of my neck, and at a furious speed I am pulled through the cold water. As I break the surface I feel a great happiness, a rush of joy. I am in familiar surroundings again, in the light, fresh air, where I can breathe and move freely. While I lie flopping on the ground, dizzy and happy, I suddenly notice Ragna's scrutinizing eye. She picks me up in her fists, holds me tight towards the sun, evaluates, twists and turns me, bends my arms and legs and neck, stretches me out, and finally pokes a finger into my stomach. From the displeasure on her face, I am afraid that my body is too pale, too thin, too small, too odd, but before I have time to protest, she breaks my neck, twists it round and throws me down to the other fish.

I'm falling and falling in the dream, but wake up at the moment my body smacks against the floor. The pain of the collision overwhelms me. Yet the surprise is worse:

to find my old nightdress way up my stomach, my pubic region dismally bared and naked, the helplessness, the gaze towards the books and the dust under the bed, the whole situation confirming the fact that I have gone down, down and under.

I'm unable to get up from the floor. I haven't had the strength for several years to get up from the floor unaided.

'Ragna! Ragna!'

She comes padding from a hiding place in the house, is suddenly standing in the room staring at me with black eyes, open-mouthed. Her jaws are working, her arms shaking; she radiates a deep urge to tie me up, to lash her prey tightly.

Clack, clack.

She is standing directly over me. Her mouth is dribbling, her black eyes glitter hungrily towards the flesh that I scarcely can move.

'Yes,' she whistles.

'Can you help me up? I was dreaming and fell on the floor.'

'Yes,' she sighs huskily, gripping me by the arm, dragging me closer to the bed, heaving in an attempt to pull me up.

'No, no, not like that, Ragna. Be more careful!'

She moans and supports herself, presses her fists in under my arms, strains, and with a sudden heave she throws my upper body towards the mattress. I grab hold of the foam rubber with all I've got in the way of hands and nails, while she, with a hard grasp round my feet, flings the rest of my body up.

I lie there in a twisted, impossible position, right on the edge of the bed, waiting for her to get hold of my bottom and push me over. I whimper, cling to the bedclothes, turn my head towards her as a sign that I am waiting for her to continue, the final lift.

Ragna stands in the middle of the floor, grinning with her mouth open. I must look a bit surprised, for now she starts to sneer and laugh, throwing her upper body forward in small jerks, holding her stomach. Her laughter does not surprise me, nor the sound of it. To anyone uninitiated, it will sound like hearty trilling. I who know her hear traces of malicious pleasure.

'Well, help me!'

The small jerks become faster; the laughter courses through her chest, builds up soundlessly before, in a final surge, it eventually bubbles over.

'Come on. Help me, then!' I cry out through the quacking din of her vocal cords.

She stops at once, puts a hand to her throat, then sneers some more. Her eyes blink and gleam, and she turns and crawls laughing out of the room, back to her hiding place.

*

I spend all my time in bed, counting neither the hours nor the days, but registering that darkness is in the process of taking over the day, the winds are increasing, the cold is seeping into the room. It must be getting on for mid-October, the time just before it starts to snow, white and pure. I feel a yearning for purity; my eyes want to rest in the white outside the window. I smell after weeks without being washed.

Ragna and I avoid each other. I call her for only the most necessary tasks. She's hardly at home at present; as soon as she has an excuse, she's over at Johan's. They're probably working together on everything that has to be managed before the winter – from the smell and the spots of blood on her clothes I know that the autumn slaughtering is under way, with freezing, hanging up to dry, smoking and mincing.

Johan hasn't shown himself since our last altercation, but Ragna is obviously back in favour – it's not only her clothes that have spots of red on them when she comes back from his place.

*

I reign as queen in my room, in spite of the dust and the dirt. I have the silence, my pen and books, and, not least, I own the hours when Ragna is away. Sometimes I listen to a programme on the radio, but generally speaking I listen and talk to myself. And that is not poor entertainment.

In this steady, calm trickle I find it easy to forget, forgive, explain away, understand. But I'm not so stupid that I don't sense the resentment beneath the everyday chores, for it's not just chicken feed that's worrying Ragna.

And I ask myself once more: Why do I want to stay? And I reply: What other choice do I have? I love the walls here, the view from the window, and will never feel at ease in the strange rooms of the nursing home, surrounded by corridors that lead to places I do not know. The insistence on adapting to all sorts of routines will be a daily struggle compared to the freedom I feel in this bed. I will be tormented by the continuous stream of people who come and then die, suffer from the noise of the physical disintegration of the old people and their death rattles, especially when I know that in this house I can wake up and fall asleep to a gust of wind or the chirruping of birds.

Coexistence with Ragna is admittedly tough, but at least it is predictable. The wretchedness has a face, a body and a language. It strikes me regularly and in particular situations, but I am not surprised, I know my adversary. I am, in spite of everything, a sister branching from the same rotten trunk.

At the nursing home, on the other hand, total annihilation threatens me. In particular I fear the attrition of my right of ownership over my own body and mind, and worry that, like some object turned into kilos, litres and diagrams, I will simply become fodder for the nursing-home hierarchy.

I stretch an arm underneath the bed, find Vol. X of *Home University*, to be more precise 'Religion, Philosophy, Psychology'. On page 84 I write, 'Assistant: She pissed on me, a litre at least. I gave her a wash and new clothes. She was wet and sticky all over! (Thinks: The old bat had a little piss in her pants, or smelt of piss at any rate. It's best to exaggerate to show how proficient I am.) Nurse: 'Excellent! (Thinks: The new patient is too demanding. We'll have to restrict her freedom to spare the other patients and carers.)'

And my sister, Ragna, has she had any other choices than this miserable stretch of land between the house and the moors, the lakes and me? What stopped her leaving before our parents died? Why didn't she send me away before I got older and more demanding?

The young Ragna, fresh-skinned and smooth-necked, maybe she walked through these rooms, full of eager dreams and wishes, with a glittering gaze fixed on the future.

She might have had her plans worked out. She would get away, go to the trading post and live in a bedsit. She probably sat in her room, thinking it all out – how she would talk and dress in order to get a job. She already had the names of people Father knew; she would surely be able to gain their trust. In a stream of images, she imagined how the first meeting would be: index finger on the doorbell, the neat pattern of her trousers and jacket against the front door, people's expressions when she presented herself as Ragna, daughter of Cloudberry Nils. Yes, they were from her family, the juicy cloudberries that were delivered to the door every August. And then she would give a slight curtsy and say that she was available for work, she could wash and iron and scrub, take care of the slaughtering and prepare the meals.

But at this point Ragna would stop her daydreaming. For wasn't it the case that she would really like to have the very finest of jobs, preferably from the start? Why be a domestic help when you could be a cashier in the food shop or a waitress in the café? Here she would meet people, become well known in the village, her face would be seen every day, either at the cash register in her orange jacket with white collar or at the tables in her white blouse and black apron, holding a burger on a plate. Occasionally, Ragna talked about this when we were children, particularly when she came home from the village and enacted all her impressions in front of the mirror in the bedroom. If I know her, she would have played around for ages with the images of herself in different roles, would have amused herself thinking about the curious looks people would give her, the long conversations that would take place among people in the village when she was finally in her position: Who is she, this new girl, this Ragna, who grabs everyone's attention with her efficiency and her clear-eyed look?

But then, in the midst of a flight of fancy, she must have realized that it would be virtually impossible for her to achieve the dream of a respectable job in the village. When I think about it, Ragna has gone on quite a few times about impenetrable family ties, saying that without exception the more well-to-do women in the village have authority over the cash registers, their daughters have been chosen for the job of café waitress as far back as their confirmation. Seen from this point of view, what other possibilities did Ragna have? She could of course have used her strength at the nursing home, for looking after people, washing and feeding them. Were there alternatives to this type of work? No, not except the home here and with me. And most likely the authorities contribute a krone or two for Ragna's care of her younger sister.

*

The question of Ragna's choices, or rather lack of choices, involves answers I am not too happy about. Her life is suddenly visible, like a stage when the curtain is pulled back. Ragna's story makes for a really uncomfortable drama, and I'm put in an impossible position when the revelation comes. There are of course all the lies she clings to so as to keep a balance between us. That she makes me weak so as to be able to feel strong herself. That she exaggerates her own importance so as to avoid feeling the pathetic, helpless female she actually is. But that I, with my need of care, have become her excuse for not creating a proper life for herself, that I and my sickly body have become her self-imposed fate and mission in life, that's something quite different. I wring my hands in despair. Yes, that's the way it is. Ragna and I are probably quite similar, have precisely the same cast of mind. We do not have any other choice but to remain. We are equally frightened and helpless, and cling to each other as a defence against the outside world: she out of anxiety about her inability to interact with other people, all the social niceties, the things she hasn't learned to master and understand; and I out of fear of losing the remainder of myself at the hands of cynical strangers in an institution.

Oh, poor helpless little Ragna, poor helpless us.

But that's not all. The truth about Ragna also contains a paradox. Profoundly and fervently she wants to be rid of me, despite the fact that I act as her shield against the world. But she feels no shame about this treachery; no, rather this innermost dark wish has helped to give her a positive image of herself. As she sees it, she is a woman who has heroically sacrificed herself for her sister's well-being for many arduous years.

I can easily imagine Ragna's refrains – can almost hear her rattling them off: 'If it weren't for your illness, I'd have had a man and children and a large house to look after!' 'If it weren't for you, you lazy layabout, I'd have been a successful working woman!' 'If it weren't for your pitifulness, I'd have been popular with other women!'

Oh yes, Ragna has always wanted to be rid of me, perhaps long before I fell ill at the age of four. For don't I have a clear picture that she reacted to my fever and crying with a strange, satisfied look? Of course, I could be exaggerating, I could be stretching the credible much too far. Even so I am open to – no, I am prepared to state that the wish became stronger when Ragna saw in advance the outcome, what would happen later, when she kept watch and took care of me for our parents: a life devoted to looking after a shabby, sickly sister out in the wilds.

So I can hardly blame her, as a child, for having tried in her own way to prevent what she suspected the future might bring. Yes indeed, that may be how it was. Why, otherwise, didn't she inform Mum and Dad when my condition suddenly worsened?

For the same reason, perhaps I ought not to judge her, little Ragna, for her cunning and her many outbursts during our childhood. And perhaps I ought not to blame her, child that she was, for all the instances of pure malice. After all, I had ruined her life with my illness.

This is one of the many incidents I ought perhaps to have forgiven:

'Ragna! Shall we pretend to be fine ladies?'

It's afternoon and we are alone in the house – I'm seven and Ragna's twelve.

I go into her room. Ragna peers at me from the bed, where she is sorting things into small boxes. Suddenly she fixes her gaze on the glass beads I'm wearing round my neck.

She gets up and comes over to me. At first I interpret this approach as friendly, but then her hand is at my throat, the necklace, and she rips it off.

'You're so horrid. And those are my beads. I'll never, ever play with anyone as horrid as you!'

And this:

'Little sister! Come here and I'll show you something.'

It's summer, perhaps a year later, and I'm sitting in the kitchen eating, but immediately I totter over to the large stone where Ragna is sitting, full of expectation.

The sun is low, so it's hard to see what she's pointing at. I bend forward as best I can, stare down into the heather.

'Do you see it? That's what you're like, precisely like that,' Ragna says.

And then I see it too. In among thin stalks and small green leaves a small mouse is dragging itself forward by its front paws; it's straining and straining, both its rear legs are broken and hang helplessly behind its little body.

And this:

It's spring and I must be nine, perhaps ten. I'm sitting on a chair just outside the front door, while Ragna is drawing patterns on the steps with a piece of chalk.

'Come and see, girls,' Dad suddenly shouts from behind the house. 'I've found a nest with two crow's eggs that are about to hatch! Hurry, before the mother returns!'

We look at each other, equally eager. I get up as quickly as I can, pull the duvet away from my thighs, grab hold of my crutches and put one leg forward. But something happens – I crash after only one step, stumble and fall flat on my face, tripped by Ragna's left foot. There's pain in my face, my arms. I look up. Ragna, running, turns round towards me, laughs and sticks out her tongue.

Our chequered relationship, all these different episodes – no, dear Ragna, I can't forgive everything. But here is a good memory, for there we are, out in the grass on a summer's day. I'm eight and you're thirteen, you're big and I'm small, you're all-knowing and I'm stupid; it's dry in the grass and dry in the air – and everything is completely still. We're sitting on the ground, on a rug, me right at the edge and you next to me. I'm fiddling with a matchbox, you're pulling up blades of grass and placing them in a small heap. We don't say much, or think much either, but from our movements and looks we reach an agreement that I am to strike a match and place it in the heap of grass.

The grass quickly catches fire, flames shoot straight up, and we move a little on the rug. But look, the fire starts to spread and crackles in the air. I become afraid and call out for you to do something. You get up and calmly ask me to roll over to the other side. I lie down, do as you say, and soon I'm on the grass, while you pull the rug up and throw it over the flames, which go out with a puff.

I smile and clap my hands, astonished. You are so quick, so sure; you are Ragna, my older sister, and you're always completely in control. You answer by laughing and tossing your hair proudly – huh, that was nothing. But suddenly you spin round. Wasn't that a sound coming from the grass, a tiny hiss, a small sigh among the blades? You raise an eyebrow, pretend to be deciding what it can be, to be devising a plan.

'It's still burning,' I say. 'Not so much, but some flickers here and there.'

'Something stronger's called for,' you shout, and pull off your pants. I stare entranced, amazed at you suddenly standing there with white legs and round buttocks in the middle of the grass, then squatting down, legs wide apart, and letting the flood descend and gush over the grass. There's a rushing, then a crackling, and look – smoke billows up into your white bottom. I point and shout, you turn round and see the same thing, and roll your eyes affectedly before collapsing in a fit of giggles. There you lie, on the burnt, pee-wet grass, with your bum in the air, and you laugh, you laugh and I laugh, we laugh and laugh. You roll over on your back, and I roll round on to my back, then we hold our stomachs and lie there, laughing for a long time in a way we'd never done before – and haven't since.

Will a memory like that save us, Ragna? Will it provide hope for a possible sisterliness?

I bang my head against the wall, confirm to myself that there can't possibly be anything else but a hard, empty shell; I can't think of anything apart from my relationship with Ragna. It's always Ragna, little Ragna, big Ragna, difficult Ragna. And I know it makes me afraid, this recognition of the fact that I live through Ragna, so I have to pinch my flesh, bore my fingers into my chest, feel the thin blood vessels burst, see the juice ooze out into the skin, become blue, almost black stains.

But the physical pain seems like small scratches on a horny surface. I can't burrow deep enough, far enough, never reach the very substance of our relationship. Our illness is too serious, the injuries too extensive, simply impossible to allow for a simple diagnosis. And admittedly I am completely inadequate to make such investigations. I lack the ability to put forward logical explanations and solutions. That's why I move restlessly among memories, moods and impressions – and that's why I can't do anything other than taste, smell and feel our chronic sister inflammation.

*

Suppose that all these episodes and memories don't exist, that there is no bitter enmity. Suppose that everything I experience is fabrication and daydreaming, and that now, tired of my notions, I am telling my story as it appears to a clear-sighted gaze – if there is such a thing as a gaze that sees clearly.

I will therefore make a tear, a hole in my life perspective, to search for a way to admit that what I experience is possibly neither correct nor true. I will be open to everything that streams out of this hole, open to thoughts that I live a quiet, simple life, a life without the dramas with which I tend to embellish every occurrence.

Can it be the radio that causes me to think in the way I have done? All these radio plays, voices that invade my room, it's possible I can't cope with them, their life stories, they lure me into believing concocted stories, into fabricating a problem from Ragna's and my relationship.

But if I have an urge to rewrite, explain away, magnify everything that happens, what then? There aren't any truths in the world anyway – well, apart from measurable facts such as length and content and mathematical formulae that no one in their right mind would question. I would argue that as long as emotions and impression and thoughts can't be expressed in diagrams, it is natural to feel some uncertainty as to what the truth of one's life resembles.

Even so, something inside me hacks away at these conceptions. A hacking that turns into a constant gnawing feeling of betraying myself no matter which conception I tend to favour. I think resignedly that I am adrift in a kaleidoscope of lies, while something inside me whispers that I can only obtain calm and certainty from examining the skeleton, the very marrow juice of the lies.

'Suck the shit out of the bone,' I say out loud to myself. 'Spit it out. Let the final truth appear to your naked eye!'

All the truth I dig trembling out of the horrible and disgusting marrow.

I, horrible and disgusting, dig all the trembling truth out of the marrow.

Yet again. All this playing around and avoiding the subject, I shuffle insights as I shuffle words, change events by changing a comma. Everything becomes drafts and sketches, no matter how I twist and turn my life.

Finally, though, after much resistance, reluctance, disinclination, I ask the questions I have never posed before:

Can it be that I, the sick one, have given rise to impatience in Ragna because of my exaggerated gestures and unreasonable demands? Can it be that I, the helpless one, have bred the anger in her by making myself more pathetic than I am? And can it be that I, in my struggle to gain the inviolable position of victim, have forged and fashioned Ragna the violator?

Furthermore, can it be that I, after years of exaggerated care needs, have robbed her of the ability to think, to create a living, inner life? Can it be that I, the crippled one, have created a cripple – a mute, empty being?

Et cetera. Can it be that this urge towards untruths is not due to my painful experiences, my dejectedness, forsakenness, but that the lies rise up in me because of the sudden love relationship between Johan and her, that I paint as black a picture of both of them as I'm able because their love threatens my leisurely existence?

If that's how it is. If that's how it really is, the marrow can only be swallowed with the mouth held close round the hollow bone shaft, and only in the deepest abyss, in the black boggy soil, can I regurgitate the confession, hold it out:

I'm the one with horns, the one with goat's eyes.

My god is oversensitive suffering. My gospels: illness and dependence. And my prayers: a constant yelping, mixed with moans and shrieks of pain.

Help me, anyone who can. I'm a woman on the periphery of all truths.

The room's ice cold. The house completely silent. Not a puff of wind to be heard.

'Ragna! I'm completely wizened with the cold!'

Ragna stands in front of me in the half-darkness, peering. Her eyes are heavy with sleep, her jaws clamped shut in a determined wish to be able to get back to bed.

'What the hell are you whining on about? And in the dead of night?'

'I'm so afraid, Ragna! I keep on thinking such weird thoughts!'

'Then get some bloody sleep like any normal person and see if that doesn't make all the madness disappear.'

Ragna is shivering and flaps her arms around her.

'You must damn well pull yourself together. Waking me up for nothing at all, you deserve a good hiding!' She hunches up even more, waves a clenched fist in my face.

I sniffle, but already feel better, almost relieved, the flickering of Ragna's white skin in the dark room, her voice, her whole being confirm that I am alive, present in the same story that I have always concocted.

*

The days leap forward, almost colliding with winter. Suddenly we're caught by crunching frost and all-engulfing darkness.

For me winter means sleep, I who am never out of the house. But at a certain point I've had enough. Through an indescribable tiredness I register the fact that I am scarcely able to distinguish myself from the bed and the dust, and as a reflex my will to live awakes and raises my body into a sitting position.

Hell's bells, I think, shaking my head in confusion.

How could I contemplate sleeping when I should be investigating the plans being made for my own disappearance?

Johan is noticeably back. From the sounds I deduce that grabbing and grubbing are going on. The winter clearly does not reduce his enormous appetite. He greedily helps himself to whatever's offered, whether it's in the kitchen or in Ragna's bedroom.

The long period of exile and the sudden awakening mean that I observe my surroundings with renewed interest. Among other things, I notice that Ragna has acquired many of Johan's expressions and gestures. She openly picks her nose and has started to blink in the same way he does. Nor does she remove her scooter outfit when she comes indoors, just lifts off the top part and lets the arms dangle round her hips like empty pistol holsters. They both sway from room to room like this, ready to be off in a shot on the scooter. They're clearly at the ready – in case something needs to be done in a hurry. But what?

I've got to admit, his company motivates me. No sooner does he cross the threshold than I start to crawl out of bed, make him aware of my presence by rattling my crutches a bit more than usual, and I totter back and forth in our corridor under the pretext of needing to train my muscles. The corridor isn't long, no more than three metres, and I can't manage many steps, perhaps sixteen a minute. But I can't deny the party feeling that comes over me when I covertly observe his expression as I painfully slowly and tenaciously pass the kitchen door: he who knows that I know that I irritate him by my mere presence, that I am so cheeky and am doing this quite deliberately, and that he can't do anything about it, except pretend that I don't exist. He's utterly annoyed. I'm maliciously delighted. That really pisses him off.

Is it at all strange that I start cackling as soon as I'm out of his field of vision, very quietly, as if I want to spare him my revealing observations? That pisses him off even more.

Oh, what an intoxicating hotchpotch of unsuccessful intentions and contrived misunderstandings!

*

Winter tightens its grip, holds us captive in a cocoon of freezing darkness and snow. Ragna spends all her time indoors; only Johan opens the front door when he comes to visit or leaves again, and then it's usually to the village to fetch news, post and food. Nor should I conceal that Johan carries in firewood. He shovels away the snow that builds up in front of the front door. He is strong and healthy, and so one could even argue that I benefit from his strength.

Compared to the open plains right outside our door, the presence of the three of us in the small house is almost claustrophobic. But that does not prevent me from getting up and making my daily trips along the corridor. This exercise, which began as an excuse, has become an important routine. It leaves me feeling wide awake and clear-headed, and confirms my position as a member of the household. Ragna and Johan, who have acquired the habit of buzzing and whispering at the kitchen table, spot me passing the kitchen door morning, afternoon and evening, back and forth, tenaciously and purposefully. As I pass, we nod briefly to each other, and I probably bare my teeth. As soon as I am out of sight, I am not out of mind; I know that the scraping of the crutches saws its way into the cosiness and warmth in there – a constant reminder of my existence. For that reason, I occasionally surprise them on good days with a couple of extra rounds.

No, I'm not so stupid as to be unaware of my hidden reasons for continually and constantly taking out my crutches. The exercise is one thing, but first and foremost the crutches are my sceptres, the power I have to create a little discomfort, to gain a little attention.

I train despite wanting to sleep and dream my time away, despite the cramp that comes after a couple of hours of rest. I massage myself as best I can, I don't want to ask Ragna when Johan is paying a visit – and that is fairly often. So after the lament of the crutches it is my sobs that accompany the sounds of the house. I don't ignore the fact that they drown everything being buzzed and whispered – in the pauses between Johan's lustful moans, it should be noted. I laugh a little and think of the noise we produce as a composition, that our voices rise and fall in a disharmonious musical score.

Yes, of course the exercise increases my strength. I am awake – and in the darkest depths of winter too!

Pain, crap, shit and piss, I shall overcome the little crutches woman at any price!

Prize pain, crap and piss, I the crutches woman shall overcome any little shit!

*

One afternoon, when the sky opens in shades of mauve and the snow appears like pink-shimmering sugar, I lapse into thoughts about the capacity of colours to create a feeling of character, of content, how they create an expectation of taste, an experience. Just as a pink sweet seems to promise to taste sweet, while a green one is almost certain to taste more acidic.

This train of thought causes me to lie there wondering what people can resemble and remind one of, everything from colours to animals and insects. Ragna, for example, I am sure resembles a wasp, for she is one in her entire being. And Johan reminds me of a special breed of dog I've seen in a magazine. He sticks out his lower jaw in precisely the same way, hard. And therefore his cheeks, like those of the dog, hang heavy and meaty past the corners of his mouth like jowls.

'Woof, woof, Johan. Doggie fetch a bone!' I whisper and laugh quietly to myself, and go on thinking about Ragna and Johan until I start pondering about myself and how I perhaps appear to other people.

'Ragna,' I say during morning care in my room on a cold day in early December. I'm sitting on a chair in front of the washstand, my face turned towards the mirror, watching her as she rubs the flannel up and down my back. After my withdrawal that lasted for several weeks she has paid more attention to my hygiene, she scrubs my armpits, lower legs and thighs every other day, in spite of the fact that I can hardly be dirty – it's more in her mind that I am unclean and grimy. So I find it suitable and quite natural to elaborate on the question I have been dying to ask her.

'Ragna,' I say again, 'what colour am I? Can you tell me that?'

'Colour? I haven't the faintest idea what you're talking about,' she replies suspiciously, and carries on scrubbing.

'I mean colour, Ragna, you know, if I'm a yellow person, or if I'm red or green.'

She laughs resignedly. Perhaps it's too early in the morning for this type of question.

'You're a black maggot, pasty and filthy creature that you are.'

'I don't mean that sort of colour, Ragna, I mean the colour I have as a person. Am I mauve? For that's what I feel I am myself.'

She wrings out the flannel with hurried movements.

'Cut out all that colour talk.'

'Ragna,' I go on trying, 'you're yellow, for example. Well, for me you are because you're always on the move, and I don't know if yellow's a colour that's on the move, but it's the colour I feel you are.'

I straighten my back, try to catch that enclosed look of hers.

'You're yellow, Ragna,' I repeat.

She rolls her eyes, takes hold of my hair and pulls it up so she can wash the back of my neck.

'What colour am I, Ragna?'

'Stop rabbiting on about that colour nonsense!'

'Yes, but I need to know! I know so little about myself – you've got Johan. And you meet people when you're in the village who can give you a feeling of who you are.'

'Oh, do shut up!'

'I can make it easy for you. I'll give you three colours to choose from: red, mauve and blue. I'm one of those – I think I'm mauve, actually. Am I? Tell me, Ragna.'

She gives a start and tugs at my hair so I feel it smart in the roots, but I don't quit, and turn towards her.

'Well, I'm mauve, then? Mauve because I am bit of an afternoon sort of person and because I think so much, isn't that right? Thoughts are mauve, Ragna, I'm sure of that.'

'Shut up! Shut up! Shut up!' she screeches, holding her ears.

The flannel dangles dripping between her fingers and produces large, angry stains on my shirt.

'You're chattering away like a crow!'

'Yes, but listen to me, Ragna – you're the only one I can ask!'

She stands there with rolling, half-closed eyes, shaking her head in frustration.

'You're not mauve, you're shit black, and that's because you plague the shit out of me! Do you hear me? Black! Black as muck! You shithead woman, you!'

Later, after my morning care, while I'm shuffling around my room, back and forth between the window and the mirror, Ragna is tidying the kitchen in a jittery mood. She stuffs glasses and plates ruthlessly into the cupboard. They must all be crammed to breaking point.

'The animal, so self-obsessed! Here am I, slaving away day and night, and all she does is think of colours! I'll give her colours, I will! Black and blue, that's what she ought to have been!'

Black or blue or mauve. It really doesn't matter. For I am in fact white. I can see that in the mirror. Almost colourless. My eyes are pale with a faint shimmer of blue, and my hair is almost completely grey – no, white. I look sort of transparent and will soon merge with the sky out there.

The colourlessness, uncertainty, everything I don't know about myself, make my thoughts slide towards images I don't like to think about. In particular, I have to think of distant, unknown coasts, places where people never cast anchor, inaccessible sounds and bays beneath ancient, gaping mountains, coasts so extensive that you see the sea curving on the horizon. They are the remotest, loneliest places in the world, they exist only on the very rim of nothingness. And I think so hard of these coasts that I get a sensation of disappearing in all the deserted wilderness – the coasts become peripheral zones of my own body, every toe, every finger points out desolately towards the emptiness in the world. I am a remote landscape so completely abandoned that I have to scream in order to feel I am alive.

'What are you whining about?' Ragna shouts from the kitchen.

'I'm disappearing, Ragna!'

'Yes, bugger off completely while you're at it, you pathetic creature!'

*

Perhaps it is the sound of the persistent tacking of the sewing-machine needle that manages to burst the bubble of the dreamy state that has kept me bedridden for a couple of days. Ragna is sewing. And it's not a question of mending or patching old clothes. No, she's sewing long tracks in large pieces of material. And when Ragna starts to hum an accompaniment to the sewing machine's monotonous clatter, I can't help feeling curious. Is she sewing new curtains in the middle of winter? Or can it be new bedlinen – the old sheets must be worn thin by all that rubbing together and physical excess?

After a while, she gets up from the table and hums even louder. I hear rustling and swishing of fabric, I hear her bustling around in the room, she is clearly in high spirits, contented. When she crosses the corridor, on her way to her bedroom, I finally catch sight of what has woken me up: from Ragna's head and down to the floor stream Mum's old lace curtains, and topping her high-piled hair, the material has been drawn together into a crown that dips over her face.

I give an almost silent whinny. That dried-up heap of bones looks no more like a bride than an old witch at a cauldron.

'Oho, Ragna, so you're getting ready for a wedding?'

'Don't stick your nose into my business,' shouts Ragna from her room, while she rummages with jewellery and clothes.

'Why haven't you told me anything about it before?'

'What do you need to know? You're only interested in yourself.'

'So, you're getting married, are you?'

'Yes. In that way we can defend ourselves against those in power!'

'It didn't exactly look like a helmet you were wearing on your head.'

'Two heads are better than one, that's what it's all about. Standing together, against all of life's threats and dangers. And that danger also includes you, don't you forget it!'

Holy Moses. I sigh and gaze at the ceiling. Up there I can for a moment escape the hard grasp that constricts my existence. I float after the pale-white colour with the utmost ease, I glide and glide and am on the point of disappearing out the vent when I am hauled back to the miserable body in the bed and slide into my own dry mouth.

'Ragna?'

'Yes?'

'Is Johan going to live here?'

'Of course he is! Have you ever heard of a married couple who don't share a bed?'

'Why haven't you said anything?'

'The wedding's at the weekend, here in this house. We want it over before Christmas. That's all been decided. Your whining won't make the slightest bit of difference.'

Despite Ragna and Johan's relationship, all their excesses, the news hits me unexpectedly. They must have made up their minds in double-quick time, otherwise I'd have already had my suspicions. But when I think about it, I'm not surprised. Yes, it's probably a wedding they've been whispering on about, imagined and planned during these last weeks at the kitchen table. I may have even provoked it by my frequent walks along the corridor, by my mere presence. They have clearly acquired a sudden need to ally themselves, yes, to have a marriage contract as a strong card to play if the situation in the house becomes critical: we decide things here!

I can't help reproaching myself. From now on 'We're married!' will ring out, scream from wall to wall and in every nook and cranny of the house. And from that day on we're divided into two irreconcilable camps: the married couple and me, we two and you, them and me.

*

Sliced smoked salmon, served with some lettuce leaves and a dollop of cream. Elk roast with French fries. Ice cream with cloudberries and Ragna's wafer cones. Red wine with the meal. Johan's home-made cowberry liqueur with the dessert.

Ragna stands by the bed rubbing her hands, looking expectantly at me. I'm invited. I'm to sit at the table. It is to be a memorable day for all of us.

Is she looking for signs of happiness? I sit there hunched up, heavy with the news, hardly able to look at her.

Later, towards evening the same day, she stands in my room once again, shakes me by the arm, wakes me from a deep, heavy sleep.

'Dear sister. Look at what I've got here! I've altered it for you. It took hours and hours. Hasn't it turned out fine?'

She holds up a dress of green burled material in front of herself. The acidic colour sticks to her face. My stomach gives a weak heave. Spittle gathers in my mouth. Has Ragna sewn on the collar and pockets? Sure to be the remains of some lace curtains. The dress must be old. I can't recall ever having seen it before. I swallow and look away.

She squeezes a clothes hanger into the dress and hangs it up on the front of the wardrobe. Perhaps so that the spirals of the white lace collar will remind me of the difficult times that lie ahead.

'Isn't it lovely?' she asks again, stroking the material with her hand. 'You've always wanted a proper dress, haven't you?'

'Yes.'

'What's the matter with you?' Ragna comes up closer, stands by the bed and stares at me suspiciously. 'You've not made up your mind to be ill, have you?'

'No, no.'

'I really hope not. It's to be my special day and you're not to ruin it!'

'Relax.'

Ragna gives a forced smile. I smile back weakly. She stands over me gleaming with a power that only the certainty of imminent happiness generates. I smile a bit more, as best I can. She breathes a sigh of relief and goes back to her wedding preparations.

Home University, Vol. VIII, 'Language and Communication', at random, in the margin, somewhere in the middle of the book: 'Marriage, damage, mad rage, bloody carnage.'

I am profoundly asleep once more when she bursts through the door with a cup in her hands.

'And how are you, dear sister – it's morning!'

She turns on the light, and in the flood of brightness I am rapidly scrutinized for all visible and future afflictions that might threaten the weekend's wedding. She puts down the cup, leans over me and straightens my pillow, pulls me by the arm in an attempt to get me up.

'I don't want anything! Just let me sleep!'

'Is that the thanks I get for coming with tea on this lovely morning?'

She presses her hand in under my arm. I have no option but to move as she wants and take up a kind of sitting position in the bed.

The teacup is placed in front of me in a hollow she makes in the duvet. She straightens up and stands there close to me. I sense that she is gazing at me with a look I do not know and turn my head in surprise to see what it is. At the same moment, my forehead bangs into her hand. There's a sting, her nails have scratched the skin, her hand is trembling. Was she about to smooth out my hair? The gaze disappears, she pulls her hand away.

'Dear sister,' she says in a husky voice, 'I only want you to have a nice day.'

'Right.'

'And you can be sure the food will be good.'

'Sure.'

'And just think, wine! For you too! It'll be a real celebration!'

'Yes.'

'The dress will suit you.'

I don't answer. She rubs her hands when I deliberately sink back into the bed. The tea slops over. A stain spreads out, I feel the heat through the duvet.

'Just be a bit pleasant, all right?'

'Yes,' I say, and turn my back to her. She bends cautiously over me, breathing heavily.

'Are you afraid?'

She's right. I've every reason to be afraid. I lie in the dark and think about curses, search for sentences that can be twisted from newlywed happiness to slow destruction, sentences that convert a good marriage into an agonizing, painful divorce. I make a pathetic attempt to write something despite my exhaustion, but console myself with the fact that if they don't work, I will make predictions, evocations, stick pins into what is about to happen:

*Ragna and Johan, kind and happy, will never meet
with cruel grief, be consumed by violent misfortune.*

*Ragna and Johan, never kind and happy, will meet
with cruel grief, be consumed by violent misfortune.*

I take a breath. Try to prevent a landslide of images that press against my forehead, the gaze behind the closed eyes. I don't want to watch these images: the cruelty in them, the humiliation, yet I am drawn towards them, yes, I observe every single shot, coolly, with distance and without dignity. Me with an axe and hammer. Ragna flung to the crows outside. The freezer full of Johan turned into steaks and ribs, mince and chops.

Everything starts swirling. I'm falling.

'Ragna! Help me!'

*

On her wedding day Ragna is up at five o'clock, stoking the stove. She hums as she puts on the coffee. Everything's ready. The pans are sparkling, the windows and walls are gleaming. I have been washed, cleaned, scrubbed the previous evening, and the meal stands prepared in the pantry, it will only need to be heated when they return from the wedding in the village.

'We'll be coming back with guests – it will be a celebration the likes of which you've never seen before!'

I wonder if she's saying this as a piece of information or a threat, but first and foremost I am thinking that I will be sitting eating and conversing with the rest of them – I've no experience of doing that, since I very rarely sit at the table and talk to Ragna.

People. The house is going to be full of people. But not more than three guests – I know that from the number of places laid out. It will be a strange experience. I've hardly seen Johan of late. He's wisely kept himself out of sight so as not to provoke a quarrel with his in-laws. The war has been de-escalated. We're to meet together on the great day in peace and harmony.

They set off into the darkness – through the window I see that Johan has fixed a flag to either side of the handlebars on the snow scooter. Beneath her capacious scooter outfit Ragna is dressed in her newly sewn dress, and her veil has been laboriously crammed in under her hood. A corner of it has escaped and is fluttering in the wind, waving to the heavens, which bless the bridal journey with a clear sky and stars.

The sound of the scooter dies away. I am left behind in a green dress.

The crows settle on the window ledge and stare into the room. The dwarf birch presses its branches against the outer wall, listening.

I collapse into a chair. Sigh wearily. Life has received me with hands that were far too polished. I glided away, slid, slipped from the good things in life as soon as I had been born. That is why I find myself in this remote corner of limited possibilities. I get up, shake my fist at this life on crutches.

Home University, Vol. VI, 'Man and Society', in the margin, at the back of the book: 'The crutches woman howls in the wilderness, screams to the sky, "This is bloody well more than enough!" The wild animals stop, prick up their ears, was that the sound of a human? But they slink on once more, it was nothing, only a murmuring of silence.'

*

From force of habit I totter into Ragna's room, sit on her chair, on her bed, open boxes and cartons, look at clothes and jewellery, all the things she collects. The red underwear is still there – a nauseating smell comes up from the box, I don't dare touch anything and quickly replace the lid. In a heap of magazines I spend a bit too long on a brochure with ladies' clothes bargains, for when I go to put it back I notice Johan's bag behind the door, the one he uses every Monday when he goes off to the village to do the shopping, to fetch and leave the post. I let out a small gasp of anxiety and enthusiasm – I must get a move on, the bag's the only thing worth spending time on. I pull it towards me: its weight doesn't surprise me, he's going to spend the next few days here – the morning after the wedding too. The bag contains both his toothbrush and a change of clothing. I open all the fasteners and pockets, examine and scrutinize everything. There's a knife and shaving things, a pack of cards and a calendar. And in a brown, worn envelope, along with some unpaid bills, there lies a letter addressed to the head nurse at the nursing home. The letter has been sealed and a stamp stuck on. Ready to be sent on Monday, the second day of Ragna and Johan's honeymoon.

There's not much to be said about what I do now, except that it takes every ounce of my strength to fetch the implements I need to open the letter and carry out my criminal act without leaving the slightest trace: a damp cloth to moisten the glue, a sharp knife to unseal the letter, a sheet of blank paper to replace Ragna's elegantly handwritten and painstakingly formulated application, an iron to flatten out all the creases and finally a little glue to seal the envelope again.

My whole body is shaking when I replace the letter in the bag. The physical overload is one thing. But the anxiety is worse. Can a blank sheet of paper, a thwarted application, prevent me from finally being sent away?

Left on the kitchen table lies Ragna's treacherous composition, the sheet with her personal request to the head of the nursing home. I quickly read a few lines, I don't need to read more, that's enough. I tear the letter to pieces and toss them on the stove; a sudden flare and the pieces turn to ash in the embers that have been smouldering there since the morning.

'…I simply can't cope any longer… Now you will have to take my sister. I'm completely worn out. She has many aches and pains and there are more of them all the time… She's not good-natured or grateful either… She belongs in a nursing home, I'm sure of that. Please fetch her, and as soon as possible. If not, you will end up having to take us both…'

Right, then, here's the final confirmation of her treachery. In a way I feel relieved. The doubt and nagging suspicion and the never-ending search for evidence have now given way to certainty. The plan has been identified, and with a clear conscience I can direct my hidden artillery against the newly married couple.

I hear the procession at a great distance, the hot-tempered snow scooters plough a path through the wood – there must be three or four vehicles. I would guess at a party of five. From my seat at the window I see that I'm right. In addition to Ragna and Johan three men are standing outside the house. They seem to be calm and self-assured, so it's probably not the Finns.

The guests move towards the entrance; the newlyweds stay standing by the scooters. They have their arms round each other. Ragna is leaning against Johan, who is clearly waiting for something to happen. I turn my gaze to the front steps, where I observe the three man take down the hoods of their scooter outfits and fish out hats from their inner pockets. They hold them between their hands while raising their chests towards the sky, inhale deeply and let out a roar of sound. It takes a few seconds before I realize they have started singing.

'May God bless our precious fatherland…' streams out from the steps, and Johan joins in with a loud voice.

'…Let folk as brothers live as one, as does befit true Christians!'

Johan's voice is surprisingly strong. I can't help but be impressed by it – it is so melodious, resonating deep within. I have to turn away. The voice tells of a power that appeals to me, one that is greater than the power that I know Johan possesses.

The front door opens: Johan and Ragna enter the house arm in arm, followed by the three men.

'Dear sister, come and congratulate us! Now we are husband and wife!'

'Like hell I will,' I say from my post at the kitchen window.

I ought to have said something ingenious, barbed and double-barrelled, but I feel confused and insulted by the letter, the wedding and all the fuss with the singing, and that voice of Johan's – why hasn't she mentioned it before?

The scooter outfits have been hung up, we've given each other a cursory greeting – hands across the kitchen table, a nod from me to each of them. Old choir buddies of Johan's, they relate, from the time when he lived out on the coast.

Ragna, the crooked catkin, stands there in the middle of the floor with her veil in folds. The men gather over by the oven, their hats are on, their chests swell, their mouths open up to the abyss within – a tide of sound streams up towards the ceiling.

It's intensely powerful. The voices take up three different levels, merging into an amazing harmony, high and low notes coil around each other and intertwine, climbing to the heights, flinging themselves down surprising slopes.

I quiver and shake, it's magic, pure seduction. I am borne aloft on the crests of waves that break, become soft and pliable. Tears fill my eyes. Where have they come from?

What an intoxicating conspiracy. I am abducted, already swept away from my rage. Stop! I cry out to myself, seize my crutches so as to stand up, go, protect myself against the lightness in the music.

The men look at me in surprise, their voices fall silent. I, too, stare at myself, down my dress, stockings, shoes. What have I done?

Ragna blushes, her nostrils flare and vibrate.

'And now it's time for some food!' she urges, turning on her heel.

The candles are burning, Johan's and Ragna's rings take turns at catching the light. I'm sitting at the table eating like the others, while a lively conversation is taking place around me. The wine is beginning to have a noticeable effect. I feel a tickling in my chest, laughter and rage bubbling and heaving away, bursting and pressing. Soon the whole works will come trickling out. Best keep my trap shut, stay away from the wine and conversation.

The nature of the men becomes increasingly clear during their visit. All of them have been made from the same mould, fired according to the same recipe: hair in a thin wisp over the forehead, belly like a sack over the trousers. They carry themselves with the same assurance, have more self-confidence than Ragna, but I note that Ragna is more authoritative. Between their legs their penises dangle – their pride and joy, no doubt about that. Like Johan, the guests seem to think they are unseen and constantly clutch their crotch, grasp the bulge with their fists, heave it outwards.

Beneath my dress hang my unfondled breasts, in my crotch lies my jewel. Have they possibly considered laying siege to me, forcing a path into my virgin territory? I'm washed and clean, my hair's been gathered into a knot, can I possibly arouse desire, do their eyes see a woman? I who have not shared saliva or juices with a living soul – what do I know about the playing of the sexes? But I have observed animals, how the ram lifts himself up, over and into the ewe, and have thought that it is impossible, impossible for me to behave with a man like that.

I can't deny it: I have pushed my chair close to the table, a bit closer to the others, and am listening attentively to the hum of conversation about the old days, about life out on the coast and their time in the choir, about the trips to Sweden and Finland and their stay in the new Russia. Here one of them was apparently tricked by a beggar into part-ing with his shoes, while another got lost and was arrested by the police, and Johan, the seducer, dispatched women every single evening. The men toast again and nudge each other, wink at Ragna – that's quite a guy she's got herself.

Ragna nods and shakes her head. At one moment she's by the stove, at the next by the table, knocking back wine in large gulps while piling meat and potatoes on to the guests' plates. Her neck muscles strain like two taut strings, she is impassive and silent, hardly a word passes her lips, only the occasional cough or guffaw escapes her throat: small wisps of smoke from the fire that is always smouldering within.

I don't like the food. The meat is tough with treachery, the gravy sour and thin with conspiracies. It is presum-ably the last meal we will share at this table, Judas wine,

Judas meal with Judas tastes – Ragna's high treason at the polished pots and pans.

After a while my back starts to hurt – I can't sit still for any length of time. A restlessness crawls up my neck, to my throat, tongue and palate. I feel an urge to rave, yes, let my hair down, throw my head back in a howl. Obviously everyone else notices my restlessness. The men don't try very hard to engage me in conversation – they've got the message. The questions go via Ragna and only have to do with the meal. Would your sister like some more potato? More to drink? Wouldn't she like some more gravy? Ragna grunts and mutters in reply. Johan sends me his watchful, menacing look, but I sit there still, behaving properly. I eat and drink, sit straight.

After the meal, the choir move over to the stove again, snap their fingers as an accompaniment to rhythmic, guttural sounds. Johan seizes Ragna, heaves her out on to the floor. Her lace crown has come away at the edges, her veil has gathered itself into a knot and bounces back and forth against her back. At last I can get up and find a place in a corner. From the periphery I watch the married couple's unstable mating dance, their ritual celebration of the conspiracy in the home. I grin inwardly – there's precious little in the way of control left. Ragna keeps on barging into Johan, who answers with jerks and shaky legs.

From the corner I also secretly watch the choir. Their bodies, the rhythm of their hands and feet, how they pull themselves up and flaunt themselves, with glazed looks and a smile around their lips. You would almost think there were more of them in our tiny kitchen, and in response to that thought my gaze wanders round the room.

Can it really be me all of them are secretly addressing? My hands search for my crutches, I tremble, keep swallowing. I'm completely unused to attention, so what am I to do? It must be all the wine, for now I start banging the crutches against the floor, keeping time, rhythmically, I don't have any choice in the matter, this is the only way I can respond to their concealed attention. I let my lips part cautiously in an attempt to smile, and immediately everything in me is flung wide open: windows, doors, shutter and vents let in roaring winds in great gusts. I am lifted, float in the air, forget my lamentable trembling body. What release. I am opened and open to everything that might take place this evening – for don't I like all of them? Every single one? Just look at them, the men, snapping, smiling – I'm the one they're singing to! I swing my body as best I can, supported by my crutches and the wall. I'm transported by their looks and my own thoughts; my hips, is it possible, I'm cautiously wriggling them – oh, God, how free I suddenly feel, here am I for real, flaunting myself! I suddenly see myself from the outside, cannot hold back the laughter building up in my chest, it's bursting out, all the resentment and restlessness I have been storing the whole evening, now it's welling up and pouring out of me.

Ragna and Johan stop suddenly. Their looks are hard and dark.

'What the hell are you playing at? Can't you behave like a civilized human being!'

Ragna is red-faced and het up, she stands in the middle of the floor with clenched fists, ready to defend morality as a newly married woman in her own home. I first think of pretending not to notice her, I'm still floating on a wave of happiness, but then I notice that the singing has died down; the men have formed a small cluster and are whispering, their backs are shaking, they are clearly trying to conceal the fact they are grinning and laughing.

The doors slam shut once more, the windows close. Something falls, heavily – well, it's my own sudden freedom lying mangled at the top of my stomach. My eyes whirl, but I straighten up. What was I thinking of, no, I'll never let myself be carried away like that again.

The men sit down at the table once more. Johan fetches a new bottle and fills the glasses. The conversation about this and that lags a bit. The mood is clearly somewhat strained. The choir give Ragna insecure looks and pretend not to see me.

I'm still standing in the corner, fiddling with my crutches, my back straight, head raised, but can't help longing for my duvet and bed. The letter, Ragna's treachery, and now the outrage in front of the choir – how much am I actually expected to be able to put up with?

Ragna shows signs of wanting to take control of the situation. The muscles in her neck tense and she tries to catch everyone's eye. But when she finally opens her mouth she doesn't start to talk about me, doesn't say a thing about her resignation, all the hard work, how difficult I am. No, she explains away again. Once more we get our story, disguised as a struggle between her and the new master race.

'We're native population too!' she says, thumping the table. 'We've lived here for ages, yes, generations of our forefathers have!'

'Yes, you bloody well have,' the choir say in unison, gazing down into their glasses of Johan's home-distilled hooch.

'And they want to ride slipshod over us – want more rights, ownership of water and the outlying areas. They'll want to own the sea next!'

'It's too bloody bad,' say the choir, taking another swig.

'We've got to stand together against the new master race. We're just as much natives as they are!'

'Sure, sure!'

'You've got to find allies as best you can – before you know where you are, they're outside the door, come to haul you out of your own home!'

'Bloody liberty!'

'They'll simply have to conform, the whole damn lot of them!'

'Yeah, are you crazy!' say the choir, banging down their glasses.

'Hey, Ragna, have you completely forgotten?' I say, crawling out of the corner.

I'm multi-armed, many-legged, stop with my sting vibrating right in front of her. The choir and Johan start, trying to chase away a sudden foreboding.

I begin to hum quietly, possibly inspired by the choir, but I have my own quite specific reasons.

'Forgotten this song?' I look questioningly at her, open my mouth wide and emit a few notes in an unsteady voice. 'You used to sing it a lot when you were young and still had a bit of flesh on you, didn't you?'

The choir and Johan look uncertainly at each other.

'Yes,' I go on. 'You knew it off by heart, and that's not so strange, for you spent a lot of time with the natives here back then – wasn't it their song, paying homage to their own history?'

Johan fidgets uneasily.

'Damn it, what's all this crap she's talking about, Ragna? Can't you get the hag off to bed so we can celebrate our wedding in peace?'

'Give it a break!' Ragna shrieks uncertainly.

'Give? If we're going to talk about giving, we ought rather to talk about you, dear Ragna. You've given one thing and another to the new master race. Do you think I didn't see you through the window here when we were young? They ran after you through the undergrowth, their pricks in their hands, as horny as hell, every man jack of them.'

'What's the pike-fish trying to say?' Johan's got up and is standing menacingly beside the table.

'All I'm saying is that Ragna has supported the new master race in her own very special way, under the warm skins, and ever since she was young. Not many of the natives have escaped her insatiable appetite for men!'

*

Home University, Vol. IV, 'History of the World', at random, somewhere in the margin: 'The sting location swelled up quickly. Deadly poison pumped into each and every cell. The victim collapsed in vomiting fits and cramps, but the antidote was quickly injected by those at the scene.

'Condition now stabilized. The poisonous vermin neutralized and carried back to its stinking cave.'

The bed embraces me, warm and soft, no one else in the world receives me in the same way – unconditionally loving and passing no judgement on my actions. I sink, fall down, but in the depths of its embrace I lie there tossing and turning between Ragna's accusations and my own defence, restless, both when dreaming and awake.

As soon as I trickle into consciousness from a moment's rest, I'm back at our trial just by registering the green dress against my skin. Was it the wine or pure malice? Or was it the actual mixing of wine and malice that produced the poison? That is how Ragna will argue and attack me. My anxiety and righteous indignation, yes, all my reasons for reacting do not exist in her repertoire of causes and explanations.

*

Johan's wedding night hammers against my eardrums. Is he punishing both Ragna and me? The chest of drawers rattles noisily against the wall at regular intervals.

I pull out two wine-bottle corks from my dress pocket that with foresight I had taken from the kitchen worktop. I try to stick them into my ears. They're too big and fall out; I've no other choice than to press them with both my hands against my head, hold them there, wait for the wedding night to be over.

Do hours pass? Days? I roll back and forth in the bed, green, poisonous, threatened with extinction.

Shame and desecration. The wedding meat is rotting on the dinner plates. In the glasses the wedding wine is coagulating. Did they cut the wedding cake and receive a small taste of their future happiness?

Ragna's face, the men's look, they appear before me at regular intervals in the darkened room. I flounder around in images from the dinner and the evening, feel lonelier and more abandoned than ever before. Even the words have gone; after jotting down my last note the books lie untouched under the bed. Possibly I can find something or other behind an old, dried-up thought, something I can scrape off and put in my mouth. But everything tastes dry and lifeless, nothing like the small sweets that make your saliva run.

*

It's early morning, the mauve tinge across the sky tells me. The dearth of words, my sleepless trial, open up a couple of memories that gradually refuse to leave me. Or have they emerged as an outcome of conscience, a desire for restitution? How else can a memory of youthful innocence assume Ragna's face and name?

I don't write anything, I detect traces of the stories along the floor, walls and windowpanes, they stretch out of their own accord, on the headboard, the alarm clock, a small figurine, only to pale and vanish once more.

Ragna, the window states. Ragna had a lovely gleam to her hair, oh yes, it flamed and burned among the green of the bushes and trees, that was what he had said the first time they met. She told me that immediately afterwards, excitedly, about his look, his voice when he spoke. Yes, she would go on and on about it for weeks and months, but to herself, in front of the mirror, in her bed before falling asleep, but always close enough for me to be able to pick up the words.

Her breath smelt strange, and I didn't like her clammy hand against my skin when she sat down on the side of the bed and told me how much in love she was; he was so kind, he had bought her a coffee at the café, and when they went outside to wait for Dad, who was doing the weekly shopping, he lent her his scarf. He was also funny; he had started to sing and laugh and nudge her as time passed and the biting north wind froze her hands and feet.

One afternoon he was, surprisingly enough, standing outside the house. He had arrived by moped along the bumpy, muddy road, and now he was standing there with mud spattered up his legs and back. I could see him from my bed; he calmly pushed down the side stand, shook the shield a bit, then took a few paces back, looked at the moped from a distance while taking his tobacco out of his pocket. He peered at the house and rolled a cigarette, but showed no signs of intending to knock or make contact. Instead, he lay down in the grass and blew out smoke in large clouds, quite relaxed, as if he had lived here for ages.

Ragna almost stopped breathing. He was right outside! And there she was, face unwashed, hair uncombed. What would he think of her when he saw her like that, a complete shambles?

She shot into her room, dashed around, hardly had time to fix her hair or change sweaters before she felt she had to go out and say hello to him. From the window I could see her face; she approached him nervously, uncertainly, and with a touch of something sweet about her mouth. He watched Ragna coming, but didn't get up, sat quite still for a moment before throwing his cigarette away and stubbing it out in the grass with his thumb, gazing at her the whole time.

From the sounds in the kitchen I deduced that Mum and Dad were ill at ease; their movements stiffened as they were suddenly like strangers in their own house. Dad coughed and started walking backwards and forwards between the corridor and the kitchen, and Mum peeled the potatoes with a gentle, alert pensiveness.

'Who is that lad? What sort of chap is he?' Dad asked several times.

Mum didn't answer at first, but while clattering with saucepans she called out that Ragna had never told her anything about it, so how could she know.

I sat down in a chair by the window ledge, well to the side, right next to the curtain, so that my interest in the proceedings wouldn't be too obvious. Dad stood watching me from the corridor, I could sense this from the silence out there and the footsteps that had subsided. When he stuck his head round my door, he didn't speak, but I knew that he wanted to express something.

I see myself sitting at the window here, see myself slowly turn towards him, silent, but with a serene expression, and I see something inside him go to pieces, there, at the door. I see what I was and could not become, all that was lost and that would grow into raging accusations, be reshaped into lonely bitterness; I can read it in his eyes from here, and I saw it the time when he was standing in the doorway, aware that there was something he ought to say.

When I turned back to the window, Ragna and the young man had disappeared. I searched among the bushes, out across the heather, behind the tree right outside, but I knew that they were already long gone when I discovered the moped tracks through the grass. I unclasped my hands – they were so cold and empty in my lap – and my legs, so tired under the chair, so unnecessary, so alien. What use was this body, what was I going to do with all this flesh, this life I had received?

'Who is that lad?' Dad called out again, entering the kitchen. 'Who is he?' he asked Mum exasperatedly.

'I don't know, I don't know,' Mum said time and time again. She had started to wash up some pots and pans.

The silence outside was enormous. I craned my neck, turned my head, pressed my face to the glass. What had become of the sounds from Ragna and the young man? Something caused me to turn towards the corridor. Now both Mum and Dad were standing there looking at me, their faces were dark, their bodies tired and worn out, and I realized, we all did, that I was one of them, the old and the useless, and that I would go on being so, for ever.

'He's sure to be a right tearaway. They're out of control, that lot,' Mum said to Dad during supper.

Her voice interrupted the silence, hard and rasping compared to the soft clinking of the cups. I was sitting over by the stove, Mum and Dad were at the kitchen table, Ragna's chair stood empty close to the table. Our glances met from time to time, but occasionally Dad banged his fist down on the table, not hard, more as confirmation of something, and then we looked at each other, briefly.

I asked to be put to bed, I had grown tired of waiting. And I also felt a sudden aversion to sitting there with Mum and Dad.

Outside the window the summer night was still light, full of promise, but I was freezing in my bed, there was a draught that I hadn't noticed before. I called for my mother and asked for an extra duvet. She shuffled in barefoot and in her nightdress. It must have already been night.

So cold. In the middle of summer. And Ragna still not back! Mum tucked the duvet round me, gave a deep sigh. Get some sleep, she said, we can't lie awake waiting, all of us.

Ragna was eighteen, at least, no one had the right to insist she stay at home. But when she did come back, many hours later, Dad was waiting in the doorway. And when he asked her where she had been and was met by silence, he demonstrated his authority by hitting her. His hand struck her on the cheek, I could hear it right out where I was, a dull thump, almost metallic. But Ragna still didn't answer, she went to bed without saying a word.

And I recall smiling faintly, and then feeling the warmth return to my body.

*

The other story I remember took place earlier, the winter when I was seven and Ragna was twelve. We were sitting in the kitchen that evening, Ragna and I, on separate stools pulled away from the table in the middle of room. We stared at each other. Mum was standing behind me with a pair of scissors in her hand, my hair was damp and she had placed a towel over my shoulders. I sat bent forward, my eyes heavy with tears. I had resisted, struggled, but was now in a way prepared, had accepted what was going to happen. Ragna was beaming, tossing her luxuriant half-length hair. It had actually already grown past her thin shoulders, but she was to be spared the scissors, left in peace, while I, with my thin, wispy hair, was to have mine cut.

'It grows unevenly,' Mum said. 'And it's so thin and fine that it gets into small tangles all over your head.'

So my hair had to be short, and now it was going to be cut off just above my ears.

Ragna sat on her stool and shone, she shone and glittered and tossed her hair, so thick, so long was it that she could plait it, gather it in a ponytail, roll it up and let it cascade down again in long, soft curls. I stared straight ahead, pretended she wasn't there, didn't take any notice of her lapping up my humiliation – Mum cutting and my tears falling at every strand of hair that gave way before the scissors.

Afterwards, I sneaked over to the mirror unseen, alone. My eyes had become so big and my head even bigger. My nature was confirmed: I was a stranger in this family and on this earth. While I suddenly realized as much, Ragna appeared out of nowhere and stood beside me. We stared at each other for a long time, from either side of the mirror, I closer, she further back. Nothing was said, but both of us saw what our reflections had to tell.

Was it the day after? No, it was several days later, and it was planned in advance – that was the only way I could avoid suspicion.

She screamed when she woke up, or rather when she picked up her brush that morning and passed it through her hair. Was it possible? During the night, the hours on her pillow, her hair had become snarled in an impenetrable ball, and it was impossible to do anything with this great clump, this thick, unruly haystack of hair all stuck together, entangled in an alarming fashion.

'God help me,' Mum sighed as she tried carefully to tease the hairs away from each other.

Ragna screamed and held her forehead with both hands, stared terror-stricken at Mum. Oh, the fear inside her – I could see it from the doorway, where Dad and I were standing.

'Oh, Ragna,' Mum said resignedly. 'I can't do anything with your hair. How could you be so stupid as to leave your chewing gum on your pillow?'

Ragna protested. She had placed well-chewed lumps of chewing gum, of the sour-tasting type she used to buy when she was in the village, on a sheet of paper on the chest of drawers, she always did that, so they were ready for the following day, still with just a little bit of taste left, and slightly hard before they turned soft and pliable between her teeth. How could they have ended up in her hair?

'You must have slept with your chewing gum in your mouth,' Mum said. 'You must stop doing that, it can be dangerous.'

Ragna is bewildered, for she has admittedly lain there chewing away at a large, good piece for too long, until the house is silent and she has almost fallen asleep, but she has definitely always taken it out. Could she have forgotten?

I stood for a while in the doorway, our eyes happened to meet for a moment, but then I tottered back to my bed as usual; pathetic and not responsible for what happened later that day: Ragna under the scissors, great lengths of her hair being chopped off, just beneath her ears, while she sobbed painfully and for a long time.

*

The self-torture continues. I am counting fears and torments. I arrive at number four: Ragna's marriage to Johan. The shame I called down on Ragna on her wedding day. The plans for my removal. The empty letter to the nursing home. In addition, there are my pains and helpless dependence. That makes a total of six. Six torments and fears. I don't know if that is a lot, but it is more than I manage to bear. My eyes feel as if they could burst, there's hammering inside my skull, my skin cracks and splits, soon the poison will explode and cover the world with darkness.

No, give me a bag, a sack, no, give me an ocean I can vomit in so I can tie all this misery up in some way or other.

After thinking all this, I have to cry for a bit, cry for everything I am and all I cannot see because of my afflictions – the greatest wonders of the earth. And what have I failed to discover in the way of beauty inside myself?

Why don't I just do the simplest thing – cut off this connection to life, a quick stab to the heart with a knife? What more can I actually hope to achieve, apart from Ragna's anger, endless days with a little food in my mouth and humiliating visits to the toilet?

But the will to live clings to the hope that something will happen, something might improve. What's more, I am a leisurely sort of person, I prefer to lie in bed dozing than to decompose completely in the earth, completely silent and devoid of thought.

*

'You spewed out lots of lava yesterday evening!'

Feet planted well apart, Johan's standing in front of my bed, thumbs thrust into the waistband of his trousers. Behind him stands Ragna, wringing her hands, her mouth is askew and twisted out of shape; it's difficult to judge if she is holding back a smirk or rage.

'Was it yesterday? I thought it was longer ago than that,' I say, and heave myself up into a sitting position to try and gain some clarity regarding the sudden visit.

'A ball of fire, that's what you were – and do you know what I propose to do about it?'

'No. Cool it down, perhaps?' I say, and scratch my head.

'This sister of yours is not at all stupid, Ragna, which is a good thing. It means she's capable of learning a lesson.'

Ragna chuckles, then stares and simultaneously doesn't stare at me. There's distance about her, a restlessness I don't like the look of.

'Fetch the scooter outfit, Ragna!' Johan shouts, glaring at me imperiously.

Ragna dashes off into the corridor and returns with one of her old outfits, stiff with oil spills, fish blood and coffee stains. She stops by my bed and holds it up in front of me.

'Now you just do exactly what we say!'

'Good grief, Ragna, have you gone stark staring mad?'

'You're going to wear this!'

'What are you two on about? What am I going to do in that outfit?'

'You're going to leave this place!' Johan shouts.

'Are you crazy?'

'You're on your way to the nursing home!'

Ragna and Johan glance quickly at each other, clearly happy with the way things are going.

'Oh, God! Ragna!' I try to catch her eye, wake her up from this madness, but she looks away and sticks close to Johan.

Johan pulls aside my duvet and throws it into the corner. The green dress has slid up and lies twined round my stomach, while my tights have slid down, revealing a cluster of hairs peeping out round the edge of my pants.

I place my hand over my crotch, keep a hold on myself in the hope of preventing the attempt to dress me that is already in progress.

'Cooperate, damn it,' Johan says, pulling me closer to the edge of the bed.

'I refuse. Do you hear? I refuse!'

'Refuse? What the hell can you refuse, you old bag?'

Ragna is standing at the end of the bed, pulling the legs of the outfit up over my calves while Johan holds me down. I try to reason with them, tense my body against the bed, but my legs and torso and arms are pushed, shoved and screwed into the outfit, to my cries and shrieks of desperation.

'I won't! I won't!'

'Refuse as much as you like, it won't do you any good,' Johan says between clenched teeth.

'Just shut up, Johan. This is something between Ragna and me!'

Johan straightens up. I'm packaged, my body lies inside the scooter outfit.

'Just in case you haven't understood, I'm the one who decides things here now.'

For a moment they stand perfectly still, exhausted and out of breath after the packaging process, but then they nod to each other, bend down over me, get hold of one end each – Johan under my arms, Ragna with my feet. I try to twist and turn to free myself, but have precious little strength in my body, except for the rage that is now growing in my chest, a violent anger that I howl out into the room, right in Johan's ear as it turns out, for he gives a start and swears, yells at me to shut up, otherwise he'll hurl me to the floor. I've no wish to collide with hard floorboards, no matter how upholstered I am, my back and legs will end up looser than ever. So I reduce my howling to a low whimper, topped by a few subdued yowls and groans.

Once in the kitchen, they lay me down on the floor. Ragna sits astride my stomach, her legs firmly round my waist, after which she grabs my wrists and presses them down to the floor, while Johan puts on his sweater and his scooter outfit.

'Now you're going to be cooled down,' she drily repeats after Johan, as if having to remind herself why she is doing this, depraved human being that she is.

When Johan's fully dressed, Ragna loosens her hold. She scrambles to her feet and walks out into the corridor for her own clothes, while Johan comes back into the kitchen.

I don't move. My moaning has died down, there's only a faint humming vibrating between my ears. Johan stares at me. I stare back. Is he going to sit on me? Pin me to the floor? But he turns his head away with a grin and at that moment I get the idea that he thinks that's what I want, that I want him to sit on my body, to pin me down.

Fancies himself, doesn't he, our Johan of the mighty voice? So melodiously conceited and fine. He's got another thing coming, then. I don't want to feel the weight of him against my body, his breath against my ear. And I start to howl again, though quite faintly.

They lift me up from the floor and carry me out of the house at a steady pace and with great care. It's amazing to make the journey out of the house with my face towards the ceiling. I spot cracks and beams and corners I have never noticed before. It strikes me that the house is still unexplored. And then I think that I ought to have spent more time studying my own home, and this immediately makes me feel more desperate, for I realize that it might be too late, from now on everything is simply uncertain. But once my head is out in the open air under the clear sky, I nevertheless feel happy that in this position I am still alive – only someone who's dead is normally carried out this way.

I register and ponder all this from a still point within myself, for all at once I realize that I have been scream-ing the whole time. I howl and scream and yell with all my might, and I'm unable to stop. I am two individuals, split and divided into an outer and an inner person, one in bewildered panic, the other calmly observing the sky above the house: I howl and marvel at the white haze up there, the unfathomable depth of the universe. I wail and wonder if everything in the world revolves around its own unsolved enigma. I scream and think: here I lie, mirroring the stars in the snot from my own nose.

And then I devote myself to gasping and sobbing. I shake and am shaken while coolly observing that I am lying on the scooter trailer in a pile of reindeer furs and old blankets. My crutches are there too, they have been stuck under my armpits; I have even managed to grab hold of one and now I am banging it rhythmically against the steel edge of the trailer. I bang away while the darkness rushes towards me, through me, while the beam of light from the scooter sweeps wildly across the wood, slicing a route along paths that only Johan knows. Branches cling and give way, lash against the trailer, I am flung back and forth in sudden jerks, but I notice that something is holding me in place. It is the rope and it is Ragna's look. She is keeping tabs, that is her job where she sits behind Johan: the leader, the seducer. Now I'm being taken away, it's final, now I am to be gone.

In the wood, Johan and Ragna are like gleaming glass – I have never seen anything of the sort before. There is a clarity that embraces them, perhaps produced by my unexpected encounter with the cold and the fresh air. I take special notice of Johan. The faint crackling across the back, the small break across the nape of the neck tell me that his substance is in the process of crumbling away in a state of constant deficiency: I haven't got enough, don't possess enough, everything streams wearily from his back as he hangs over the scooter. So much that just disappears, all the time!

And I see the repressed suggestion of goodness in him, that which he has never dared make use of for fear of losing it – it lies inside him like a half-rotten fruit, unusable except for his own nauseating interests.

That is how it is with most things. Even the wood stands there pouring out its troubles: the winters are far too long, the summers far too short, the sun and the heat never stay long enough. And so the branches become knotted and stunted.

Time disappears – I don't know how long we have been going, but we're now through the wood and approaching a flat, wide-open area. Some way out, Johan stops. They get off the scooter, waddle towards me in the dark, thick outfits, undo the rope and pull me off the trailer. They drag me across the coarse surface: it is hard and cold, I am laid down and take a look around me. The white surface stretches endlessly out into the darkness. I am probably on water that has frozen solid.

Johan and Ragna are standing over me nudging each other, grinning. Ragna is bent over double, holding her stomach; the laughter is welling up in her. It's on the point of gushing out.

'Now all you've got to do is cool down!' they shout out, and walk unsteadily away from me, bending over with suppressed salvos of laughter. The scooter is started with a jerk and they set off towards the wood. They shout and yell into the angry roar of the vehicle; there is an echo of power over the entire expanse of water, but gradually the sounds die away, not unlike the humming of mosquitoes up under the ceiling, and then, all at once, I'm lying there alone, sucked into the silence.

I've never lain out in the open before, my face to the sky, except in my first year as a baby, and then secure in a pram or a box. And if I ignore my stay in hospital, I have never been so far away from home before.

It marks a turning point to lie outdoors like this, yes, it's a ground-breaking act in my otherwise uniform life. That's probably why I keep lying there in silence, without a word on my lips, why I lie stiff and motionless on the ice. The sky above me is overwhelming. The vast reaches of space up there, which I never think about and have never really sensed, now appear to be filled with countless possibilities and dizzying explanations, as I suddenly realize what life is. My life is.

What darkness. And what reality: I can choose to see myself in a completely different way. And do so just by changing angle, altering the perspective for my, up to now, so limited, yes, horizontal observations and reflections.

And then I think of all that's been wasted, that I could have been so many other things than the 'crone on crutches' and 'catkin in the wilderness'.

But a new life is still conceivable, feasible, merely by virtue of being alive. I can transform myself via a multitude of images and explanations, it is perfectly possible – just by shifting my body a certain distance away, to the nursing home, for example. How might I not view myself from there? Won't I, the self-obsessed and troublesome one, be seen as a likeable fellow human being among all those pig-headed senile old people? Won't I, the pathetic and helpless one, appear strong and independent among those who are even weaker? And won't I, the sickly sister, stand out as being healthy and almost young among ancient women with death in their bodies and their look?

The cold fills the outfit. It's tight around the shoulders, back and hips, makes my legs feel more withered than ever. I start to shake. But it is not only the cold. I am shaken just as much by the sudden revelation, this confirmation of something important has been recognized, by the prospects of change, a different existence. And when I realize that the revelation coincides with this sudden limitation of being left abandoned on the ice, I see the possibilities and the finale, so to speak, at the same time, and the shaking increases and becomes more violent. My teeth chatter uncontrollably, my muscles quiver in intolerable tension, my stomach contracts in a way that makes my back arch into a U.

Is what is happening to me true? Can it be something I am fantasizing in my vivid imagination? That's what Ragna is always saying, time and again, that my ideas have no basis in reality. But if this isn't real, then what is? A dream, an explaining away of my life that is so endlessly hollow I have to fill it up with bizarre, strange stories in order to feel a grain of happiness, a little excitement, anger?

The sky, the darkness, the stars in infinite space: no, I'm not hollow. I'm full of possibilities and the strangest experiences.

It's probably the laughter I hear first of all, but it could just as well be the noise of the engine, the sounds mixing and increasing in strength as they come nearer. As they leave the wood and reach the edge of the water, I distinguish Ragna's jerky laughter from the roar of the engine, her hoarse, crackling laughter; she must have laughed the whole way.

I have my back to them and can't see them. When the engine is turned off, only their footsteps tell me that they'll soon be right next to me. They don't exchange a word and remain silent for a long moment when they finally come to a halt.

'Sister,' Ragna says, clearing her throat. Her voice is thin and piercing, it must be after all the screeching. 'Sister?'

I don't know what she sees, how can I, locked solid in the still point into which I have fallen, a point from which the water, the wood, Ragna and Johan are seen astonishingly clearly? I would have liked to say something, confirmed my existence to her, but not a sound comes out. And when I try to grip round the edges of myself and clamber up to the surface, I don't move. I am completely lost in myself and cannot budge for sheer peace and serenity and an imperturbable laid-backness. But through the clarity that surrounds me I notice that I am physically shaking, I am shaking so strongly, so violently that Johan moves a step, he gives ground, and behind him is the wood, and under him is the ice, and above us all is the sky.

Johan bends down and places a hand under my armpit, the other under my knees, and then he lifts me up in a single movement. He holds me to his chest, moves with firm steps towards the trailer, and all the time Ragna trips after him, places a supporting hand under my bottom and calves. But she's not much help. Johan bears my entire weight, and not only my weight, he has to hold tightly on to my clattering body with all his might so as not to lose hold – I am shaking that much in his arms.

They lay me down in the trailer with great exertions and groanings, try to lay me down flat, but my U is unbreakable, unsnappable. Finally they agree that Ragna will sit beside me and hold on to me. She clambers up into the trailer and settles down, places her arms tightly round my stomach and calls out, 'Ready,' to Johan, who cautiously starts the scooter, and then we take the same route home.

*

The trip back under the blankets, being carried into the house and the warmth of my bed.

The pain of the slow thawing out is intolerable. I enter into a long parenthesis – white lines page after page in *Home University*.

Everything is a daze and void, until the moment when someone places something on my bedside table. A dull sound, fresh air.

I look up from my pillow. Ragna is there; she has just put down a dish of sliced fruit.

'Eat, dear sister. You haven't touched any food for days.'

I gradually wake up to the life that has been foisted on me. My heart beats in the cavity of my chest, my blood courses through my veins, my flesh is warm and tangible. No doubt about it, I am still on my journey through time.

I register my existence with a certain fatigue, have no expectations about what use I can put it to. It must be because death has stroked me with its cold fingers, the frost that has so painfully been driven out of my bones and joints. My eyes in the mirror. The only thing that will continue, that happens all the time, is the decline and slow disintegration of the body.

Not until I have almost recovered my powers do the memories of the experience out on the ice return. From my exhausted, half-withered position, the revelation out there seems fainter, not quite as feasible. Furthermore, there is something about the home's same old boards, the knotholes in the ceiling beams – everything is as before, and radiates the feeling that my life ought to continue precisely like that: immobile, still.

My head sinks back on to the pillow. There is nothing more to think about.

*

I freeze and shake, sweat and drowse in turns. Hammering and thudding fill my head, my entire body. Yes, I am in the process of waking up, that's what must be happening. And that's good, particularly because words have announced their arrival. They run around in the room unrestrainedly, and under the bed sentences have begun to collect in large, dirty heaps. So it's time to roll up my sleeves.

I stretch out a hand, try to grasp some word or other, but they react by huddling together into unpleasant, hurtful sentences that stare at me from the corners of the room and the wardrobe. I don't like it, throw a pillow at the nastiest ones. But I shouldn't have done that, for suddenly they come at me and insist on a place in both my head and the bed. I flounder around in 'abductions', 'marriage' and 'nursing home', can hardly breathe, and it's no good trying to catch them, for they immediately grow short-tempered and red and even bigger.

I say to myself that I must relax, breathe, pretend they're not there. But the number of words just increases, they come streaming in, and suddenly they start to propagate into 'abhome', 'marductions' and 'nursinges'. To avoid chaos and panic I have no other choice but to make room for all of them – I realize that they simply ought to have their own, chosen shelves. I work feverishly, sorting and clearing away at great speed, place 'abhome', 'marductions' and 'nursinges' at the bottom, but realize immediately that that won't work out. The old words start falling down when I place them on the shelves, their labels have gone and soon I don't even recognize any of them. I examine them from all sides, every one of them, shake out their contents, but that too is a false move – everything gets mixed up together and splits up into new and even more incomprehensible meanings.

I gasp for breath.

Ragna is standing by the bed, staring at me. She places a cold cloth on my forehead – as if that was necessary; the whole pillow is soaking wet.

Her look: the fear within, it's not hard to work out that it's got to do with me.

*

Ragna moves round me with a new, strange attentiveness. I don't know if I like it or not – it may well be that Johan affects me with his outbursts.

'What the hell's going on, Ragna?'

Ragna has left the stove and her simmering saucepans and entered my room without any warning, without a single call from me. I'm lying under the duvet in a dreamy doze, listening absently to her approaching steps. When she is close, I look up from the pillow, but she doesn't say anything, only opens a drawer, takes out a comb and, without a single word, starts with determined strokes to fix my hair. She is breathing close to my ear, short puffs. I try to wriggle free but she keeps a firm hold by gripping me round the forehead.

She goes through my hair several times, the unaccustomed strokes seeming to burn my scalp. Then she stops and removes the loose hairs from the comb.

'There, now you look a bit better,' she says with a distant smile, opens one hand, rolls the loose hairs into a small ball that she takes with her back to the kitchen. Once there, she opens the stove door, and immediately afterwards I can hear the hairs crackle as they are consumed by the fire.

'What the hell are you up to now, then?'

Ragna has suddenly, without any warning, without a single call from me, got up from her game of cards and entered my room. Once inside, she starts to tug at my arms even though I'm asleep, and without any explanation hauls me into a sitting position. She presses my upper body forward until I hang dangling over my thighs, keeping me in that position with a supportive hand while starting to shake the pillows with the other. She shakes and bangs and pokes them into position, and when she's finished shoves me back again. I seem to be a bit stiff, but that's perhaps because I'm uncertain what she's really up to. She doesn't answer my quizzical, half-tired look, just strokes the clean bedlinen with one hand, and is out of the room again.

'Ragna! What the bloody hell!'

Even though I haven't rattled my crutches, called out or moaned, Ragna leaves the dinner table and comes into my room. My cold and congealed food stands untouched on a stool placed next to the bed. The spoon is sticking up out of the porridge. This has been going on for many days.

'What a lovely dinner!' she says, clapping her hands together.

I don't answer. How can I counter her words with my non-existent appetite? Possibly she interprets my lack of response as approval, for she sits down on the edge of the bed and leans towards me, the bowl of porridge in the crook of her arm.

Ragna is suddenly much too close: her smell, skin and the heat of her body. I turn my face away. She immediately interprets my gesture as a refusal to eat. And so I turn my head back and she quickly pushes two spoonfuls into my mouth.

'You can't do without food,' she says, following up with a third.

I protest, mumble with my cheeks stuffed that I'm not hungry, that I just want to be left in peace.

'Is that all you have to say to your kind sister? You ought to be ashamed. Here I am preparing all this lovely food and even spoon-feeding you with it!'

'Yes, I know, Ragna. The food's fine, it's just I'm not hungry.'

Ragna studies me for a moment in silence. She stares at me with a worried frown. I try to smile, would so much like to tell her that I'm quite content now, but just as I open my mouth to do so, she shovels in another spoonful. I chew and chew with tears in my eyes, cannot do anything else, my protests are all long since gone.

'There, that's a good girl,' she says. 'You'll see, it'll all turn out fine again.'

*

Kind, considerate Ragna.

Cool air streams towards me from a gap in the window. Low light falls into the room and spreads out over the floor. The sun is once more on its way towards the sky and life is returning. The blackest time of year is past, Christmas is over, yes, even my birthday in January has passed by unnoticed. I have lost several weeks from illness and a fever, it must almost be February, everything is airiness and light – and it has been streaming towards me for several days.

The world is new and open. I've got new bedclothes, the room smells fresh and the dust is gone from the corners. Fruit is placed on my bedside table every morning, cut into small pieces, to suit my stomach. A glass of water is served at the same time. I have to drink it while Ragna stands watching me.

One morning, the taste of the cool water makes me remember the experience out on the ice; the thoughts I had about myself under the sky, yes, the actual revelation about the limited, yes, straightforwardly horizontal nature of my life.

I drink the water, swallow it down, and nod, smiling cautiously at Ragna. She opens her mouth, revealing her teeth as an answer. In this state of awakening and purification the possibility of leaving her exists. I can let the single gaze remain in this room.

*

Ragna searches through the clothes in my cupboard. She pulls out one piece of clothing after the other, two, three old dresses, a pair of trousers, some jackets, takes them over to the window, squints and holds them up, examines the seams, sees if the material has any holes.

She divides the clothes into two small piles. Some items are obviously to be thrown out, I can sense this from the way she kicks them away. Others are to be mended, and a few of them washed. There's no limit to the consideration she is displaying at present. It would seem to be a good opportunity now to talk to her about my decision:

'Ragna,' I say from my bed, well propped up with pillows. 'There's something we must talk about, something that happened out there on the ice.'

'There's nothing more to talk about, that's all over and done with.'

'But Ragna, I've got to talk to you about it.'

'There's nothing more to be said, we've finished that discussion.'

'We haven't talked about it one little bit.'

'You behave properly and you'll see that everything works out all right.'

'Yes, but Ragna, I don't want to have it like this any longer.'

'Well, things will be different in future, I can tell you that.'

'I mean, it could just be that I want something else.'

'You're always wanting something else. Making trouble, that's the only thing you're good at.'

Ragna's attention is on the clothes; it's difficult to tell if she has realized my genuine need to talk, the words come out mechanically, she simply churns them out, in the same way that she churns out meals when she's busy.

*

I must talk with Ragna before the letter with the blank sheet of paper is returned, before she announces she's heard nothing, before she phones the nursing home and asks what's become of their answer – her application was sent ages ago.

What application? the woman in charge will ask. We haven't received any letter. I'll check to be on the safe side, but I'm absolutely sure we've never received an application for your sister to be admitted. What address did you send the letter to? Well, that's the right one, the street number's correct, strange, the postal service never mixes things up normally. When was it sent? Really? No, all I can suggest is that you send a new one, and as quickly as you can, and in the meantime we will try to find out where the mistake has taken place, yes, and what can have happened to your letter.

'Ragna!' I try again several days later when Johan is out of the house and she is close by, in the bathroom to be more precise, where she is down on her knees scrubbing the floor.

'Do you think I'm a good human being?' I call out from the bed into the corridor.

'You should be glad you're as healthy as you are,' she calls back.

'I mean, do you like the person I am?'

'You're much too preoccupied with yourself. There are more important things to think about. Many people are far worse off than you are.'

'So you really think that I'm just a lot of trouble? You don't like all the caring and nursing?'

'What I don't like is all your fussing. You have a tendency to yap away about things that don't exist.'

'Perhaps it would be best if we just went our separate ways?'

'I didn't say that. All I'm saying is that far too much of your talk consists of lies and imaginings.'

'But Ragna, it's the way I see the world, it's how the world is to me.'

'All well and good, but a lot of what you see isn't right.'

'How can you know that?'

'Because so much of what you think is such utter nonsense!'

'So there's never any nonsense in your life?'

'No, I really haven't time for that sort of thing. Stuff and nonsense, that's you, you lazy little beast!'

Ragna has got up from the floor, her last words drowned by the sound of water being emptied into the washbasin. The discussion is clearly over for the time being, I can feel this from the way the bucket is slammed into the cupboard. Even so, I'm surprised. When did Ragna and I last have such a long conversation?

*

Ragna's care of me becomes increasingly cursory as soon as I feel a little better. She spends nearly all her time with Johan; they sit in the kitchen playing cards and drinking coffee, unless they happen to be discussing politics and the apportioning of water and outlying areas. The daily routines are interrupted only by Johan's sudden lust and some scooter trips to the village.

Towards the end of March the sun causes large patches of wet grass and mud to appear. The main roads are already dry, I hear them say, and after a short while the snow scooter is replaced by Johan's motorbike.

The change of transport is an occasion for great rejoicing; they yell and shout when the bike picks up speed in the wet earth and skids on slush.

From time to time, she mends my clothes. The sewing machine hammers away over loose seams and open holes, and she mends stockings, pants and socks by hand with needle and thread. When the clothes are washed and clean, she hangs them up on the outside of the wardrobe, and smaller items destined for the drawers she places on the chest of drawers. Nothing is put back, everything is left out, eloquently expressing how much Ragna does for me.

The battle for the toilet has died down – as far as I'm concerned, at any rate. My long stay in bed and the draining exhaustion of my convalescence have meant that I have to relieve myself in the chamber pot that Ragna places under me in the bed. And perhaps that's just as well. There wouldn't have been enough time for us all in the morning, with Johan sitting there for an hour at least.

Several months after the wedding, it turns out that Ragna has the same impatience with Johan that she used to have with me. She turns the light off and on when she feels he's been in there too long, kicks the door, or just leaves him inside in utter darkness.

'Johan, you prick!' she shouts. 'Hurry up, will you?'

But, unlike the sharp tone of voice she uses with me, she talks to Johan with playfulness and laughter in her voice.

Johan swears and curses in there, rummages around with clothes and paper, and when he finally comes out, sweaty and all worked up, it quite often happens that he flies straight at her.

'Bloody woman,' he sometimes says, and drags her off to the bedroom for punishment and an encounter with his dipstick. Accompanied all the time by Ragna's laughter – ecstatic, gleeful.

And then the sounds of them die away, plugged and shut out by the wine-bottle corks I press against my ears. Sealed off in my hermetic universe, I still sense the bitter sweetness of the wedding wine, and hear the hatred inside me that rushes back and forth incessantly, redder and bloodier than the thin liquid that squeezes through my veins.

*

Johan is seldom – practically never – inside my room. And now that I spend all my time in bed, he is virtually invisible to me. Although we do sometimes catch sight of each other when he passes down the corridor, on his way to the bedroom or the toilet. From time to time, when I'm in form, I sometimes bend forward a little and turn my head precisely when I hear him coming. For a brief instant, we let our eyes rest on each other, but I always take care to pull myself quickly back with a short, derisive clatter, well before he can pretend anything, and before he can bore through me with that murderous look of his:

Stupid cowardly Johan with his voice, forcedly
good, pretends first that I am nothing,
afterwards kills the crutch woman with his look.

First I the crutch woman am nothing, afterwards
I kill stupid cowardly Johan, pretend nothing
with my look, my voice.

The sentences just work. I've achieved the meaning I wanted. At last I can once more carry on my most precious occupation: lie on the pillows and twist the world exactly as I like.

*

'Well, sister, and how do you like your life as a newlywed?'

For several days, Ragna has been attacking the house with cloth and water along the walls and skirting boards and ceiling. Now she's standing on a stool in my room with her arms in the air, rubbing the cloth quickly back and forth over some black stains just above the bed where I am lying dozing under the duvet.

'None of your business,' she groans.

'Well, you're enjoying it, aren't you? I can't remember when the house has ever been so clean.'

'You're being cheeky and sarcastic, I refuse to answer.'

'There's life in the old bitch yet, it would seem. Perhaps there'll be children, you know, from a second biblical Sarah? Small Johans and small Ragnas crawling around and peeing all over your newly washed floors?'

Ragna turns round suddenly and flings the cloth into the bucket so the water splashes everywhere. But I can't stop myself.

'Johan's clearly working away at it, though, isn't he? I mean, that's what he's devoting practically all his energy to at the moment, wouldn't you say?' I send her a questioning look.

Ragna jumps down from the stool with a crash, leans over me and shakes her fist.

'Shut up, you whiny old cow! You're just jealous – you've hardly any juices worth stirring in your carcass!'

She dries her forehead, breathes heavily. Black sweat stains have spread out under her armpits. Ragna has never liked spring-cleaning, but she always keeps going till she's finished, room by room, with an untiring zeal. Now she takes the bucket with her and leaves the room with a taut neck and a clenched fist that she bashes into the door frame.

'She's on the mend, the old hag,' she calls out from the kitchen.

Johan makes approving noises in his throat, though absent-mindedly, as he's playing patience.

Home University, Vol. IX, 'Health, Welfare, Economy', on a white area near the end of the book: 'No juices, eh? I see, I see. I've turned sour on old bile, vomit and repressed body fluids. What can one do about that? Well, a man's pure medicine of course. No, thanks all the same. I've seen the side effects: loss of wits and control. I'd sooner turn sour and end up a foul-smelling troll.'

*

Johan and Ragna's married life has made me wonder about the relationship between man and woman. Or rather, what such a life can do to a woman, and even more precisely, how the relationship has changed Ragna. The trance-like clashes that end with the infiltration of Johan's sexual organ into hers, all the beast-like sounds she utters during the act, that's one thing – she who has always hated my instinctive nature, who wants to discipline all my sudden whims. But what really surprises me is that Ragna, this obstinate, unaffected woman, more and more frequently is transforming herself into a two-headed non-independent We.

'Ragna,' I might call out in the afternoon, 'what are we having for dinner?'

'There's blood sausage with sugar.'

'But Ragna, that's not the sort of food either of us likes to eat!'

'We've already decided what's for dinner. You're going to have to eat the same as us!'

'All that blood makes me constipated!'

'Stuff and nonsense! We don't notice anything!'

Or: 'Ragna, what on earth? All that noise in the middle of the day?'

'We're listening to a music programme on the radio!'

'That's not at all like you!'

'None of your business, you jealous bitch. We like it a lot!'

Or: 'Ragna, will you remember to return my books to the library? And perhaps borrow some new ones?'

'Well, no. I mean, we've got lots and lots of other things to think about.'

'But can't you split up for a bit? So you can do your own errands?'

'No, we don't feel like doing that at all!'

Over the years, I've had a great deal to find fault with regarding Ragna's particular nature: her stubbornness, her fiery temper. But these characteristics have also represented her strength: the raw force that has enabled us to cope on our own in this home. Ragna still asserts her ideas with vehemence; she is not afraid of picking a fight with Johan and defending herself and her opinions. But in spite of that, We is the strongest party in the relationship – when anything is asserted from that perspective, they turn gentle and tractable as kittens, both of them. A crackdown is launched on the one who lets this third party down, the one who tries to break and take a different tack. For that reason, it isn't hard to imagine what they talk about in the kitchen, all the comments and arguments aimed to stabilize the holy We alliance.

'Why aren't you concentrating, Ragna?'

'I was just thinking I ought to take the chamber pot away from under my sister.'

'We're in the middle of a game of cards. You're not her bloody slave, can't it wait?'

'That's true, Johan, we'll play until one of us wins.'

Or: 'What am I to do, Johan? She's wearing me out. And you never help me either.'

'It would be bloody marvellous if the two of us lived here alone.'

'Yes, Johan, and we will someday, you'll see.'

Or: 'How about a ride on the motorbike?'

'My sister's still not quite well yet. I ought to be here and take care of her.'

'I'm so bloody fed up. You can't go on behaving like this. Soon you're going to have to choose. It's us or her.'

'Relax. Obviously I'll choose us!'

*

One afternoon I have a dream that's so strange I wake up with a start. The images are unusually clear, the experience so vivid and strong that I go on lying there with a wide-open, fixed gaze until it gets dark.

I dreamt I lay trapped under the ruins of a collapsed house, I was half-suffocated and close to death, under a huge pile of stones but with an air pocket close to my nose. And I wasn't alone, there was someone else in the ruins, just as half-dead as I was. When the house collapsed, we had managed to get hold of each other's hands, we lay separate and hidden by the rubble, but our fingers were intertwined. I didn't know who the other person was, but I had a feeling that it was a woman, and that there was something familiar and close in the contact between hands and skin.

We held on to each other for a long time and signalled via squeezing and tweaking that we were still alive – a reassurance and encouragement for both of us.

But after a while the other person's squeezes grew slacker, colder, the hand responded more weakly and less frequently to my squeezes, and finally stopped altogether. I tried to stretch the other person's fingers, make large movements with my hand to get a reaction, but stones and the position of my arm made it impossible. Finally I had to accept that the other person was dead and that I was completely alone in the ruins of the collapsed house.

I cried, and in a way that was a good thing because the tears sealed me off, I could abandon myself to grieving for what I had lost, and the fact that I was lost to life. I cried until everything went pale, almost white, and it was then that the strangest thing in the dream happened. The rubble was lifted off my body and daylight streamed towards me. Blinded, happy, I held my hands in front of my eyes; right above me I could make out the contours of a figure, a man, and when he bent down and examined my injuries, I felt even happier, for I was sure that we knew each other – I just didn't know where from or how. I made a sign that I wanted to be lifted up, but he didn't touch me, only shrugged his shoulders resignedly, and he then left me in the ruins with quick, light steps. Just before he disappeared over the horizon, he turned round and waved, and it was then that I woke up.

If only I understood what the dream meant, if only I knew who he was, why he didn't want to take me with him. These are the questions I am struggling with when evening comes and Ragna is standing at the foot of my bed.

She stares at me sceptically.

'What's up with you? Have you seen a ghost?'

I don't answer, but blink several times to try and escape from the hypnotizing images. I shake my head uncomprehendingly, look a bit worried, lift the duvet. And then I understand, I can feel it in my whole body – the pain in my back and thighs after having lain lopsidedly and in an arch over the chamber pot. It's a relief when Ragna removes the po, but at the same time it causes me violent pain as my back sinks down into the mattress. I've been lying there for several hours, at least.

The pot sloshes and splashes, Ragna makes a face and holds her nose.

'What a stench,' she says, and quickly spreads the duvet out over me.

*

The days come and go. From my inert life on the pillows I have plenty of time to study the married couple's rhythm of daily activities.

Every morning starts like this: Ragna puts the coffee on. As soon as it's ready, Johan comes to the kitchen table and they drink cup after cup together while they natter away and laugh. And after having drunk a whole pot, they boil another one that they also immediately drink. Along with these cups of pitch-black gritty coffee they eat large slices of bread that Ragna has baked. Or rather, Ragna prods a few crumbs into her mouth, while Johan wolfs down whatever is going from her full plate. After that they sometimes go back to bed, and when they get up an hour later, it's more coffee and perhaps some card games and patience. This is the basic structure of their everyday life, everything else is a variation, but the variations also have a familiar and predictable pattern: a motorbike ride somewhere or other, shopping trips to the village (when Ragna is with him, these always include a visit to a café), or surprises, such as a fishing trip to one of the lakes not far from home. When they come back, it's time for coffee again. Maybe they will also listen to the radio; that can lead to a discussion and even an argument. But after a spot of reconciliatory activity, in either the bedroom or the bathroom, everything's fine again. Sometimes they can spend the entire morning in bed, and they can stay in the bathroom for hours. But those are the rare exceptions.

Of course they take a certain amount of time mending things, clearing up and doing housework. At regular intervals Ragna does the washing, while Johan chops wood.

Ragna bakes and irons, while Johan fixes the vehicles and repairs things round the house. Just before he's finished, he will step into the kitchen and rub his hands, then give an affected shiver.

'Ah, a little coffee wouldn't be a bad idea, I think,' he might say, and so he will take a well-earned coffee break.

Naturally, Johan and Ragna's chores are seasonal. Now it's spring and there's little to be done. In autumn they will trawl the moors for cloudberries, will fish and hunt and smoke and mince, and then sell most of what they have gathered to other people and various outlets. But if I have understood their marital conspiracy right, they take plenty of breaks and have lots of cosy times together, completely oblivious of my presence and my unsatisfied needs.

*

'Ragna!' I call out one afternoon, my voice perhaps unnecessarily sharp, but it's because I feel up to things and much better. 'Ragna!' I call out again. 'Have you remembered what I asked you about?'

Everything goes quiet in the kitchen.

'What's that, then?' comes the piercing reply after a while.

'Books,' I say sternly, my voice out of control. 'Why didn't you bring any home last time?'

I can hear them moving around uneasily in there.

'Books?'

'Yes, books. At the library. It's ages since you were last there.'

'What a bloody fusspot,' Johan says quietly, as if to himself.

'It's really too bad.'

'You've been ill,' is Ragna's immediate reply. 'You ought to be glad you've recovered as well has you have!'

'Yes, all right. But now I'm much better. And I need something to read.'

'Books! Books! I've spent every single moment of my free time on you. And all you can do is complain that I don't fetch books for you?'

Ragna bangs a glass down hard on the table. I hear her get up and rattle the cups around in the sink.

'All you think about is Johan and yourself.'

'Don't you bring Johan into this. He's got more than enough to lug around on his trips to the village. It's not exactly nothing, all you put away. And on top of that you want him to carry books for you!'

'Don't be stupid, Ragna. You know what I mean.'

'What you mean is just rubbish. And let me tell you one thing.' Ragna bangs her hand down on the draining board by the sink: the cups clatter, there's rattling in the cupboards. 'Not a book is going to enter this house until you're more grateful for all the things I do for you!'

Ragna lets out a pretend sob. She even snuffles.

'The bloody harridan,' Johan says under his breath, then gets up and walks over to comfort her.

*

Johan is sitting in my chair. And it's my place at the kitchen table he takes all day long. He's taken over my time in the toilet, and steals much of the attention and care I otherwise had from Ragna.

Johan has got things as he wants them. I have been banished to my bedroom, thrown out and reduced to a gaping hole that has to be fed and emptied, while my head's hunger, my need to read and write, is ignored and ridiculed.

I'm shaking, my jaws are in the process of crushing each other in anger the likes of which I have never felt before. Of course I can move out, become a piece of furniture at a nursing home. But! And at this *but!* I feel my jaws press together even harder: I would never have had the idea of leaving this house, my own particular spot in the world, if Johan hadn't moved in, if he and Ragna hadn't teamed up and doubled my troubles in this home.

I reach for my crutches. No, despite the revelation out on the ice I don't want to leave one bit, not yet at any rate, and not before I have tried to turn the situation around. I count my lucky stars that Ragna has realized my decision, otherwise Johan would never get the punishment he deserves.

Isn't it my cup he still lifts to that huge mouth of his? My plate his greedy fingers eat from?

*

There are various jobs that need to be done. But the project is of such a nature that I keep it to myself, I don't say a single word about it in *Home University*, don't formulate it for my inner gaze or ear, except as a magic spell, a hoarse incantation: tish, vish, vush, vish vanish…

All previous plans are put on hold, now there are other priorities: up out of bed, from my withered, will-less sickbed – that's of the utmost urgency. But it's not training I trust my luck to, the crutches' complaint across the floor, no, it's the collecting of paraphernalia, of small crucial items that will help me attain my goal.

Slowly, slowly I raise myself from my pillows, lift the duvet, and slowly, slowly I get out of bed. I am panting, sweating, feel dizzy from all the blood hammering away in my chest, but eventually I am standing upright on the rug.

My thighs, hips and stomach are a quivering landslide since my bones can hardly bear their own weight. I reel, and have to hold on to the side of the bed; the floor resembles an undertow beneath my feet.

Right, then. That's the state of play, that's how things are right now, and this is how it has been many times, it's just a question of getting a good grip on the crutches, gritting my teeth.

*

'Damn it, straight into the jaws of hell!'

Johan makes a quick-tempered move at the sudden sight of me in the kitchen doorway. The shock is probably due to the fact that after several months I am once more standing upright in my own house. My hair has probably tangled itself into great big knots and the state of my nightdress and the way my body smells have been affected by my long stay in bed, even though my sister has been attentive in caring for me.

Ragna gawps at me, absent-mindedly puts down a jar of preserves.

'Are you crazy?'

'No, I'm much better, and I want to be up for a bit!'

'Dear sister, you're still not well. Go back to your room and at least let me help you change into some better clothes!'

'There's no need. I'll just sit here for a bit – it's so long since I've been in the kitchen.'

I push Ragna aside as she rushes towards me and totter slowly, moaning, over to her empty chair, right opposite Johan. The chair receives me with a loud grating noise; the chair legs scrap across the floor. It really does hurt to sit on a chair, my hips don't like the unaccustomed position. But I am convinced that this is what is necessary, in addition to the various things that have to be collected in order for me to carry out my assignment.

I can't help laughing to myself. Both of them are clearly confused. Ragna places a cup of tea in front of me. I spend a long time putting in the sugar, stirring, and letting my hand shake affectedly.

I am the centre of attention, but I pretend not to notice, drink the tea slowly, study my nails at length, give a long yawn with my mouth wide open; a belch even emerges from the depths of my throat. Ragna has started to clear up in the larder again, Johan is laying out cards on the table. Then suddenly he stands up and walks into the corridor, starts to rummage around with his outdoor clothes.

'Ragna! Shall we go for a ride?'

She turns and looks at me uncertainly. I stir my tea absent-mindedly, take a sip from the cup, stare out into space.

She is silent for a short while. Then she says loudly and abruptly, 'Coming right away, Johan!'

Good. Couldn't be better. The couple have once more been reminded of my existence. For the time being, their married life will continue in the presence of my unmistakable physical existence.

Collecting all the things I need proves easier than I had anticipated. As soon as they are out of the door, I check the kitchen table on Johan's side, my former place, and, yes, there I find three thick, black hairs that must be his. I place them in a matchbox, grab a glass and totter slowly but surely back to my own room.

I put the hairs in the glass, place it on the chest of drawers, and if I'm quick – relatively speaking, in my condition – I can manage to get hold of some more. My heart is hammering, I'm in motion, I cackle and pant in turns, it's a matter of time, of life, yes, a particular one.

In Johan and Ragna's room it's obvious where Johan sleeps. I've worked it out from the sounds already, but the clothes also make it clear: Ragna's shiny red nightdress sticks out from under the pillow on her side. As best I can, I bend over Johan's sheet, supported on a crutch, running a nail over the sheet, lifting it slightly, to collect the bits and pieces from his body in a small heap. I sneeze, my nose blocks up: it must be flakes of skin and dust swirling around in the air. But there, right beside his pillow, I discover what I am searching for, the curled, short form, the hardness: a hair from Johan's private parts.

There's no need to try and explain away what I am up to. Something has to be done and this is my means of doing it. But, to be honest, I don't like it. In horror I witness myself tie a knot in the hairs, then place them in the glass together with a sheet of paper on which I have written Johan's full name and the most horrible sentences I have ever concocted. And with loathing I see myself place a lit match to the piece of paper and the shameful contents and watch them flare up, and even laugh out loud when everything has turned into ashes.

Tish, vish, vush, vish vanish... tish, vish, vush, vish vanish... The moans, the booming in the voice; with amazement I hear the sound and the words come, I am lost, entranced by my deeds, I do it automatically, my reason gawping from the sidelines.

And I go on. I don't want to stop. The hate in me brings the glass out from its place of concealment behind the bedside lamp, gets me to spit three times into the ashes; soon it will be morning.

Why all these qualms, these questions of right and wrong, when I know that every day from now on, nine days in a row, I will continue my ritual with incantations and sorcery, and finally pour the filth where it belongs – down our communal toilet?

No, spare me lifted fingers and sensible talk. The sorcery has already produced results: after only one day I have a feeling of control, the sense that my curse can affect developments in the house. Furthermore, the ritual has a soothing effect on my sudden need for companionship – I do not feel the urge to share a table with the married couple more than absolutely necessary.

As soon as I get a chance, I lie happily fantasizing about what will soon happen. What will happen to Johan is also not insignificant. The various phases of the transformation can take place gradually or quite swiftly, but that doesn't mean all that much – it's the result that counts. I have no doubt that some of my wishes might be a bit excessive for a single carcass, that it is not possible for all of them to be fulfilled, but on the other hand I enjoy thinking about them, so much so that I lie under the duvet shaking with held-in laughter at the images they conjure up.

In one of the fantasies I see the pair of them in Ragna's bedroom, where Johan is lying pale and half-dead in the bed.

'I can't understand it,' he'll say. 'What's happening, Ragna? Look at this!'

And he'll loosen his belt and pull down his trousers, quickly, so as not to lose her interest.

'Just look,' he'll say again, and jiggle his hand inside his pants.

He'll stare wide-eyed at her, with a glazed look, trying as best he can to ensure her sympathy before he shows her his wretched state.

'Well?' Ragna will ask, with a touch of impatience in her voice. 'Let's see, then.'

Johan will slowly pull his pants down over the back of his hand, slowly reveal what he is holding between thumb and index finger.

Ragna will raise an eyebrow.

'Yes,' he'll interrupt, his voice in falsetto, before she has time to say anything. 'It's unbelievable.'

Ragna will lean forward, wide-eyed and shocked.

'Can't you see it?' he'll ask nervously.

'Yes, of course I can,' Ragna will reply, full of astonishment.

'Doesn't it look like your sister? Can you see it? It's bloody well got her face!'

Ragna will feel faint. What a horrible transformation, what a fate for the poor man. I, with my peering face, will grin at him and her, remind them of my existence, in all their moments of pleasure.

If I know Ragna, she will quickly work out the consequence of what has happened. She will slowly straighten up, perhaps purse her lips and glance disapprovingly at the deformed manhood, but will then without any mercy decide that Johan must move back to his own house and that henceforth he cannot be used for anything other than hard physical labour.

*

A month passes, then a couple more weeks. The sun rolls across the sky around the clock, without ever touching the horizon – it's already the middle of May.

The tree outside my window now has small, light-green buds, and fresh shoots are sticking their heads out of the thawed ground: grasses, heather and the first tentative beginnings of what will become rosebay willowherb in large mauve clusters.

One Monday morning, just after breakfast, Ragna decides to accompany Johan to the village. I sit at the kitchen table eating – a daily self-imposed chore so that I can better study the state of the master of the house. Unconcernedly, half turned away, I minutely examine him as usual for signs of the imminent fall: a worried look, a sudden movement of the hand, a marked loss of zest for life and desire. But he seems as untroubled as ever, feet planted wide apart, scratching his nose, and there seem to be no other horrors lying in store except for some bruises on his backside from all the potholes in the road.

I am not worried, consoling myself with the fact that everything in this world takes time. Just look at the spring outside the window. It slides slowly towards fulfilment, almost imperceptibly. The mere thought of my secret, treacherous deeds makes me feel as light as a feather – springlike, pale green.

Ragna has noticed the change, my good mood, and has been surprisingly gentle of late. Before they leave, she actually bares her teeth slightly, a small, encouraging smile that tells me to take things easy until they get back. As soon as she is out of the door, I slap my thighs, laugh and chuckle to myself: If only she knew what I have been thinking about for the past few weeks.

Finally, at last, I am alone again – it's been too long since the last time. I snuggle down in bed among the soft pillows, the warm duvet. How nice to be undisturbed in the house, so marvellous not to be a source of trouble or irritation. I let out a cautious *I exist!*, try again, louder: *I exist!* The room shakes with my power, with my presence, and I confirm that I own myself right from the tip of my tongue down to my withered toes.

*

I'm woken by Ragna and Johan standing staring at me. They've still got their outdoor clothes on, the return trip must have been cold – her nose is dripping. Their looks: I don't like their looks. Something must have happened to me while I was asleep. Have I have come out in a rash, a tumour, something frightening? I quickly sit up, check the skin on my arm, touch my face, but all seems normal.

'What is it?' I say with a sudden dryness in my mouth.

'What is it? You dare ask?'

Johan and Ragna glance briefly at each other. Johan is biting his lower lip and Ragna is breathing out quickly through her nose.

'Yes?' I attempt.

Johan stretches out an arm. Before I have time to see what he is holding, Ragna grabs it from him, brings it right in front of my eyes with a quivering hand. She doesn't need to tell me. I know from the sinking feeling in my stomach, the dizzying sensation that knocks all the air out of me and presses me down into the bed.

'What's this? Can you tell me that?'

Her hand is so thin, the sinews and veins wind their way over the bones, and her nails are so sharp, they bore into the blank sheet of paper that is crumpled between her fingers.

'Answer then, damn you. I've no more patience left. Answer!'

To underline that she means business, she grabs one shoulder of my nightdress, shoves me hard against the wall.

'For a while things were quite all right,' I answer weakly, rubbing the back of my neck with my hand.

'All right? They're bloody well not all right. It's all pure obstinacy on your part.'

'You don't understand. For a while I wanted to leave, but then you refused to talk about it.'

'What's all this bullshit? I only want a straight answer: was this you?' She holds the ball of paper up in front of me once more.

'In a way, yes. I didn't want to, but then I did, but now I don't want to any longer. And it's your fault.'

'Don't want to any longer? My fault? Explain yourself a bit better, will you?'

'Yes, it's your fault. You never listen to me.'

'My fault! My fault! Are you out of your mind – am I the one responsible for the letter arriving like this?'

She opens her hand around the crumpled piece of paper, smooths it out with quivering hands, displays the evidence in front of me.

'Yes, if you'd been a bit more open, we could have talked about it.'

'Talked? All you've got to do is explain how this blank sheet of paper got into the envelope I sent to the nursing home.'

'But first you have to listen to me.'

'Your excuses aren't worth wasting a second on.'

'You've got to. I can't stand all this quarrelling.'

Johan has caught sight of the glass behind the lamp. He wrinkles up his nose, examines the contents with obvious confusion.

'What the hell is all this muck, Ragna?'

Ragna turns round quickly, stares angrily at the glass Johan is holding.

'It looks like some coal-black filth,' she states.

He raises the glass up to the light in the ceiling, turns it round and round; the light can't filter through the thick black ooze, but some flakes of ash sticking up betray its contents.

'What's the old cow been burning? And what did she put it out with?'

Johan sticks his nose into the glass. He grimaces and pulls away quickly again.

'What have you been burning?' Ragna asks.

'I don't know,' I say, swallowing.

'There are the remains of some writing here!'

Johan pokes down into the glass with a finger. Ragna seizes the glass, glares at the contents, turns slowly towards me, disbelievingly, her mouth open.

'Oh, my God. You burned the application. You've bloody well gone and burned the whole of my application to the nursing home!'

I'm about to protest, but immediately realize that it's almost impossible to come up with a simple and plausible explanation that Ragna might believe. I twist the duvet around me, start to babble about trivialities to give myself time to concoct a story both of them will accept. But a glance in Ragna's direction tells me that she sees my babbling as a sign of lies and evasion. She yawns loudly and rolls her eyes, is pale and clearly in a state of shock, grabs the collar of my nightdress with both hands, twists it round hard, presses me down into the bed.

My incoherent babbling stops. I am shocked, me too; quite simply, I cannot think of anything that will explain the pitch-black contents of the glass. A wave of panic rises in my throat. I realize that I am hoist by my own petard, that my future hangs on an impossible choice between two explanations: burning the application or casting a spell on Johan.

I try to move so I can breathe, catch Ragna's gaze, but her hands respond by twisting my collar even tighter. My mouth feels dry, useless; I can't get any air past my lips, any word out of my mouth. I want to swallow, but can hardly move my throat. The only thing I do is think, while my breath bursts and bangs in my throat, *Poor, poor Ragna, I have never seen you so furious before in my life.*

III

Back in the attic

Three hundred and sixty-five million years ago, at some point during the late Devonian and early Carboniferous periods, 70 per cent of all life was annihilated. A hundred and fifteen million years later, during the transition between the Permian and the Triassic, the same thing happened again, but this time 96 per cent of life in the sea and 70 per cent of life on land died.

After a seething, breathing, surging, pounding life of reptiles, amphibians, plants, insects, invertebrates, practically everything disappeared in an instant, or perhaps slowly, over time – but a time that we can't count, a time that does not exist, a time that relentlessly closes around skin and shell, bone and cartilage. Leftovers that also gradually crumble, disintegrate, are gone, for even the decomposition ceases, after a time there is hardly anything left to decompose – not a morsel, a stub, a scrap, not even a sweeping of what was once a great diversity of existence, can be detected in the ocean or on the surface of the earth. Even the dust of what once lived is gone. Everything has collapsed into a slough of oblivion, layer upon layer beneath crusts and in hidden cavities. Disappeared into an infinity of stillness that, using the human numerical system and human concepts, spans a period of *several hundred million years*.

That is how it continues, unceasingly.

Life comes into being. After one mass extermination then another, after life has emerged and disappeared, re-emerged and disappeared once more, after death upon death upon death in an infinity of time, you arrive at the form of a human being – a species among many other species – developed in the course of a few hectic thousand years. Your limbs are long, wobbly and thin, flesh-pink, and you have no shell, bristles or feathers. You belong to a species that walks on two legs, is carnivorous and equipped with a cunning intelligence that, among other things, manifests itself in a desire for dominion over other animals and nature. And you are aware of your own finiteness, the definitive, the ineluctable.

That is the certainty into which you are created and by which you are created.

The activity of the earth is death. The smell of the earth is death.

You turn your face away. Close your eyes, hold your nose. The putrefaction, the disgusting, nauseous filth of the earth, is something you can't stand.

You want to live.

*

I don't want to be gone. I don't want to!

Hasn't that always been my mantra? My obsession throughout my life?

Perhaps I managed to live on only air and thoughts. I'm still here, although somewhat reduced and in an unknown part of the house. I can't recall, so to speak, whether we have an attic, a whole floor above the kitchen and our bedrooms. I can't remember either a staircase or a door that leads up here, or ever hearing Ragna on the stairs, rummaging around in the crates and boxes, or being aware of steps above the ceiling when I lay in bed in my old room. Something must have happened since our last clash, Ragna's rage must have completely taken over. She pushed me down on the bed, that much I remember, but not how I was brought here, transported up the narrow staircase. I don't understand how they managed; I was probably unconscious. She must have hit me, and she must have hit me hard – large portions of my memory have been blanked out.

I want to go down again, to my room and bed and all my books. I want to go down and live to the rhythm of morning, afternoon and evening. Is it day or night? The day cycle has ended, summer is at its most intense, I can't sleep and I'm not completely awake either. The sun, this burning light, everything has become so white – it must be due to the height, I have probably never been closer to the sky. I am constantly blinded, can hardly see, everything in this room has a reflection so penetratingly white that I have to screw up my eyes or keep them completely shut.

It tires me out so much. If only I had a pair of sunglasses. 'Rgna!'

'Rgna!' I try again. 'Iv gt t hve sm snglasss!'

The dryness in my mouth glues the words together until they're almost unrecognizable. I haven't drunk anything for several days. Or is it weeks? Under this burning sky, completely outside time, it could just as well be a question of months, if not years, orbiting in an insane thirst around the sun. Ragna must come immediately with thirst-quenching water – if not, it will be impossible to bring me back to life. For I am already a dried-out country lying here. I am earth so dry that I have cracks several metres down into the abyss. At the bottom, in the depths down there, I continue to trickle – a thin, seeping stream that slowly twists along its bed, waiting for rain, for floods, for the balm of Ragna's care.

But time is short. Sand blows in across the plains, fills cavities, drifts into the cracks. Only the tongue and palate are still working in this godforsaken body, and they are both in the process of swelling up into the sky.

'Cm, Rgna! Hlp. M so thrsty!'

How can she suddenly avoid all contact, bound as she is by her obligation as a sister to take care of me? The sudden idleness after her lifelong, daily activity must, if nothing else, have given rise to a feeling of unrest, or gnawing thoughts about how I am getting on now. What does she do with her time? Does she feel a twinge in the morning around the time for my morning care? Does she wake up at night around the time I used to call out for help?

Johan has sabotaged our sisterly pact, he's the one who's lured her into thinking new thoughts, making choices that distance her from her true work. What does he really want, that greedy man-child? For her to wash and dry his bottom, the same as she did previously for me?

*

This room, it seems impossible to think that anyone can have lived here. The house was built before Ragna was born, but everything seems to be worn out and dilapidated. The paint on the floorboards has been worn away in a straight line from the bed to the door, probably by someone over a period of years. The curtains, faded and threadbare, flutter by the draughty window, while on the walls the sharp outlines of frames suggest that pictures once hung there. The chair, the bedside table and the chest of drawers wobble on unstable legs, the water has been turned off at the mains and the washstand is cracked. I can't understand it; someone must have lived and worked in this room, but not Ragna or me, and it can't have been Mum and Dad either.

There is no reason to doubt my location, where I actually find myself, for right beneath the window the old birch tree stands swaying. I could grasp the branches if I wanted to, and see, when I stretch towards the glass, how the rosebay willowherb grows in great clusters as before, and how the open plains stretch out in their familiar way for miles and miles around. Everything is as usual – both the view and the room, just dilapidated, and seen from high up. And that makes me feel really giddy.

Time is spent in bed, as before, except that the mattress here is hard and resists when my body presses against it. I miss sinking into soft pillows, and I miss my daydreaming; I pass nearly all my time lying with my eyes half-closed, peering, turning a bit every now and again, and without all that many thoughts in my head. I know that I ought to be up training, get hold of my crutches, take the few steps over to the door, perhaps as far as out into the attic room and over to the stairs. I was eager to begin with, but then I was still full of hope of an imminent reunion with my former life on the ground floor.

I have also raged and created havoc around me; occasionally I scream horribly and bang my crutches against the furniture and the wall. Ragna and Johan then react with stillness, whispers, and the pent-up laughter stops completely. But the stillness never lasts for all that long, they're too happy in their newly won freedom. I can see them in my mind's eye, sitting at the kitchen table when it happens; looking at each other and praying silently that they can last out: sooner or later these terrible attacks of rage of mine must come to an end. If not, surely they would have come up here, seen how I was doing, blessed me with some water and some care?

No, nothing's as it should be. This violent shifting between surges of strength and exhaustion, I don't understand it; sometimes I am consumed by a fuming rage, and this despite my insane thirst and my physical state. The surges of strength come suddenly, I've no idea from where, but it's probably natural they start to grow in intensity every time I think of what's happened – that I've been dumped and forgotten by both of them. It starts as a slight tingling sensation, a touch of resentment; perhaps I feel the longing for Ragna's hands. But the surges increase under the heavy weight of everything that has created my screwed-up life. And they grow even stronger and more violent when I think of what Johan has set in motion.

At some point or other it's as if I lose all control, and it's difficult to say if the surges come from inside or outside me. Everything is seen from the outside, I am reduced to an observing eye, I stare at myself and my actions, matter-of-factly, neutrally, from a place in the corner here. I see myself arch my back, I see my arms, the muscles quiveringly taut, and then I see myself thrust forward with my feet, lift my body with my lower legs, my thighs, hold myself upright on powerful legs. And in this way I stand in bed, like a mountain, and roar.

Yet what surprises me most is not the surges of strength or the lower body that in an instant starts to function. No, it's what happens the following morning or night, or perhaps just a few hours later (what do I know about the cycle of day and night in this eternally burning light?). Twice it's happened, and on both occasions after an attack: I wake up and discover that the furniture is not in the same condition as before, or rather, the furniture that I smashed, destroyed during the attack, all the discarded things that I pulled out of boxes and suitcases in the attic room outside – they're gone, every single thing has been removed and tidied away. There's not a strip of paper to be seen, not a trace of splintered wood, not a scrap of razor-sharp glass shattered into a thousand fragments visible anywhere.

The last time I lay down on the floor, I even sniffed, smelt, examined things; bored my eye down into every single crack along the length of the floorboards. A grain of dust, a strand of hair, a little dirt here and there, oh yes, but not the trace of the mirror or the washbasin that I had just smashed to pieces. The mirror dust, the millions of small mirror particles, ought to have been winking up at me in the light, glittering in brief flashes and all the colours of the rainbow. But the floor was swept clean of all traces of my outburst. Only the wall where the washbasin and mirror had once hung confirmed what had happened. Yes, that's right, it's absolutely true – I stood up and went over to that corner of the room, on my own legs, surely and steadily. And I bashed my crutches against the porcelain and the glass until everything was in ruins around me. The turned-off water taps that now jut out into the room, the marks on the walls from the crutches, there can be no other explanation: it's true that the washstand and the mirror have been here, and it's equally true that every little piece of them has gone.

True?

If I sucked the marrow from my bones and spat it out, the very core of my innermost being, then perhaps completely different truths would be revealed, come gleamingly to light. It is all fantasy, a product of my endless life in bed, lost in aimless daydreaming as I always am. Daydreams with night in them and with nameless moons and planets as homes for a mind that's gone astray.

But I fear the worst, that which is worse: that I am dying and approaching final annihilation, yes, that I'm in the middle of an apocalypse, in its shining, swelling nucleus.

I ought to be prepared. I've always been aware of the fact that sooner or later it will happen. I am, in spite of everything, someone who has lived at the furthest extremities of life, and I experience these extremities daily, inside the walls of this house. The lopsidedness of the chair, the dull sheen of the glass, the fatigue in everything and everyone, I have constantly observed the frailty, visible proof of the fact that nothing ultimately endures in the struggle against the forces of destruction. Disintegration, cessation – I've lived with the threat every single day: death quivering in a cup, in a step, in a single action, in the slightest movement. The things around me and I have realized that death can come at any moment, just a wrong step, a small slip, and the cup is broken and I am gone. It's got nothing to do with my helplessness, my dependence on crutches, but is simply due to the unpredictability of death.

*

So perhaps things have come to this: I am perhaps close to annihilation, while they sit downstairs enjoying their coffee. It's unbearable, for Johan is sure to be squirming in pleasure on the chair where I ought to have been sitting, and munching away at cakes I ought to have been eating. And Ragna, who ought to have been busy nursing and caring, is probably sitting there right at this moment, flaunting herself with her blouse open and her breasts bared. It is shameful how they are enjoying good food and each other while I'm left lying abandoned and unsure whether I am alive or dead. And just to make it quite clear once more, I still do not want to be among the dead.

So what else is left to me other than to rage: bang on the floor with my crutches, shout out their names, yell the filthiest words I know, and finally smash the chair and bedside table. But no matter how much racket I make, no matter how much I hammer and wreck the place, it will only ever be a faint clinking compared to the noise of the rage that thunders deep down within me. And once again I end up just as uncomprehending, confused at what later happens: the scraps of wood that made up the bedside table are gone, as are the remains of the chair – there's not a splinter left. So now the room is empty and completely clean, and all that's left is me and the bed. But of course we are also inseparable, forever bound to each other.

*

I seep and trickle, murmur like a tiny stream at the bottom of life. I get the idea of undressing, folding my clothes neatly, placing them on the pillow, going out into the small streak of water, dipping my head into the silvery liquid and quenching my thirst on the very last vestiges of life inside myself.

Maybe I ought to just stay lying like this, motionless, let the water run into my eyes, nose, fill my mouth, lungs, lie and let my thirst be quenched, and then trickle away, become part of the water, gleaming and transparent: the ultimate confirmation of my invisible life.

And perhaps, still with my face in the water, I will see two sentences come floating by. That is the final judgement, the punishment for everything I have done in my struggle to become visible to Ragna and Johan. I have to choose between the two, there is no fixed ending, no forgiveness, my existence will continue, depending on the sentence I choose:

I exist, and do not know it.
I do not exist, and know it.

*

'Cm, Rgna! M blddy thrsty!'

But no, Ragna is not to be budged, she remains downstairs with her resentment and anger. She has consistently ignored my cries, all the racket and my supplications. She wants to have me gone, that's nothing new, she's wanted that for ages. The nursing home is one thing, but during the slow progress along my dried-up riverbed, among the remains of my joy in living and urge to live, I have brushed up against this and that: an impression of her here, a memory there, small events that confirm that Ragna already wanted me gone when she was quite small.

But perhaps it isn't the case that my sister at long last wants to see me disappear, for maybe I have not been created, incarnated, indeed not even rendered intelligible as an idea in this world. Here, right at the beginning of memories, I am open to the idea that I, this dusty old thought of living, this primeval wish for a life, have not been conceived and born.

Everything is so confusing, what is it that is actually happening? Is even my own death, this inexorable cessation that has always seemed to me to be a clear, ineluctable truth, to become just as full of uncertainty and speculation as my entire life has been? I can feel that it exhausts me, I am so endlessly tired of never knowing, never completely understanding, of constantly finding myself, no, being forced into an endless series of guesses and assumptions. Maybe there is no forgiveness; after annihilation waits not a final explanation, no reconciling peace, just new enigmas and an infinity of possible answers.

Does the spell that I tried to put on Johan produce those surges of sudden strength, but in the wrong direction, so the words, the filthy, contemptible words that were meant for him, are actually striking me instead, their sharpness slowly twisting my thoughts and draining my strength?

*

The books, the scribblings under the bed in my old room: I would like to have written down what I think and experience, but perhaps writing is precisely what I am doing? A narrative about two seedy sisters and their determined struggle for a life, but also about all of us who have lapsed into laziness and fantasizing, hidden away in a room closer to the sky than the earth?

Therefore, when I finally let go, loosen my last connection with the secure, the usual and the general, it can of course be explained as the result of my craving for drama, my desire to lie and rewrite and change everything that takes place. For here I come, on a free fall through the Cambrian, Devonian, Jurassic, Cretaceous, tumbling through the primeval sky, primeval time, time before, time when, time after, *the time has come*; receive me, hold me, I am a poor grizzled one, a newly hatched one, or perhaps nothing.

'Hlp! Rgna! M dsapprng!'

But it is not Ragna's hands I can feel, it is the pain from stone and sand, earth and roots pressing against my back and chest. And it is not her voice I hear, reassuringly telling me to pull myself together, but the sound of regular spade-cuts that gradually fall silent. And it is not Ragna who disappears out of the door, angry and furious, it is time wrapping itself around skin and skull, bone and cartilage. And it is not I nestling under the duvet, it is I lying abandoned in a mire of oblivion, just next to the birch tree, right outside my old window. And it is not I fishing a book up from under the bed and placing a pen between my fingers. It is I who have no more to write, no more book to fill, not a margin, not a page to compose. Everything has been written, my story is complete, it disappears. And in a moment I will be gone.

Peirene

Contemporary
European Literature.
Thought provoking,
well designed, short.

'*Two-hour books to be
devoured in a single sitting:
literary cinema for those
fatigued by film.*' TLS

Online Bookshop

Subscriptions

Literary Salons

Reading Guides

Publisher's Blog

www.peirenepress.com

Follow us on twitter and Facebook @PeirenePress
Peirene Press is building a community of passionate readers.
We love to hear your comments and ideas.
Please email the publisher at: meike.ziervogel@peirenepress.com

Subscribe

Peirene Press publishes series of world-class contemporary novellas. An annual subscription consists of three books chosen from across the world connected by a single theme.

The books will be sent out in December (in time for Christmas), May and September. Any title in the series already in print when you order will be posted immediately.

The perfect way for book lovers to collect all the Peirene titles.

'A class act.' GUARDIAN

'An invaluable contribution to our cultural life.'
ANDREW MOTION

£35   1 Year Subscription (3 books, free p&p)

£65   2 Year Subscription (6 books, free p&p)

£90   3 Year Subscription (9 books, free p&p)

Peirene Press, 17 Cheverton Road, London N19 3BB
T 020 7686 1941
E subscriptions@peirenepress.com

www.peirenepress.com/shop
with secure online ordering facility

Peirene's Series

SMALL EPIC: UNRAVELLING SECRETS

NO 7
The Brothers by Asko Sahlberg
Translated from the Finnish by Emily Jeremiah and Fleur Jeremiah
'Intensely visual.' INDEPENDENT ON SUNDAY

NO 8
The Murder of Halland by Pia Juul
Translated from the Danish by Martin Aitken
'A brilliantly drawn character.' TLS

NO 9
Sea of Ink by Richard Weihe
Translated from the Swiss German by Jamie Bulloch
'Delicate and moving.' INDEPENDENT

....
TURNING POINT:
REVOLUTIONARY MOMENTS

NO 10
The Mussel Feast by Birgit Vanderbeke
Translated from the German by Jamie Bulloch
'An extraordinary book.' STANDPOINT

NO 11
Mr Darwin's Gardener by Kristina Carlson
Translated from the Finnish by Emily Jeremiah and Fleur Jeremiah
'Something miraculous.' GUARDIAN

NO 12
Chasing the King of Hearts by Hanna Krall
Translated from the Polish by Philip Boehm
'A remarkable find.' SUNDAY TIMES

COMING-OF-AGE: TOWARDS IDENTITY

NO 13
The Dead Lake by Hamid Ismailov
Translated from the Russian by Andrew Bromfield
'Immense poetic power.' GUARDIAN

NO 14
The Blue Room by Hanne Ørstavik
Translated from the Norwegian by Deborah Dawkin
'Shrewd and psychologically adroit.' LANCASHIRE
EVENING POST

NO 15
Under the Tripoli Sky by Kamal Ben Hameda
Translated from the French by Adriana Hunter
'It is excellent.' SUNDAY TIMES

....
NEW IN 2015
CHANCE ENCOUNTER: MEETING THE OTHER

NO 16
White Hunger by Aki Ollikainen
Translated from the Finnish by Emily Jeremiah and Fleur Jeremiah
'A tale of epic substance.'
LOS ANGELES REVIEW OF BOOKS

NO 17
Reader for Hire by Raymond Jean
Translated from the French by Adriana Hunter
'A book that will make you want to read more books.'
COSMOPOLITAN

NO 18
The Looking-Glass Sisters by Gøhril Gabrielsen
Translated from the Norwegian by John Irons
*'Raw and dark and wonderfully different from anything
else.'* DAG OG TID

Peirene Press is proud to support the Maya Centre.

The Maya Centre provides free psychodynamic counselling and group psychotherapy for women on low incomes in London. The counselling is offered in many different languages, including Arabic, Turkish and Portuguese. The centre also undertakes educational work on women's mental health issues.

By buying this book you help the Maya Centre to continue their pioneering services.
Peirene Press will donate 50p from the sale of this book to the Maya Centre.

www.mayacentre.org.uk